A BEACH DESTINY

KENT CLINE

authorHOUSE®

AuthorHouse™
1663 Liberty Drive
Bloomington, IN 47403
www.authorhouse.com
Phone: 1 (800) 839-8640

Published by AuthorHouse 06/25/2018

ISBN: 978-1-5462-4747-0 (sc)
ISBN: 978-1-5462-4746-3 (e)

Library of Congress Control Number: 2018907198

Print information available on the last page.

ACKNOWLEDGMENTS

Thanks to Jackie Goudeau for typing my manuscript. I had hand written it so you were a tremendous help. You are a blessing and a wonderful friend and neighbor.

Thanks to my sister, Marlys Thompson for all you do for me.

Thanks to my best friend, Ken Reeves, for proof reading my manuscript and also for allowing me to use his computers and copier at his office.

Thanks to Rachel Shoemaker for helping with all my computer problems.

A huge thanks go out to Chandler Dudley for designing and drawing the front cover. You are such a talented artist.

DEDICATION

To my children, Jennifer and her husband
John. To Kyle and his wife Stephanie.
To my three wonderful Grandchildren, Ayden,
Ella, and Hudson.
Love from Papa Kent.

CHAPTER 1

Kevin woke up around 7. His four friends were all snoring and sleeping off their hangovers. He fumbled for his shorts and tennis shoes, grabbed a t-shirt and quietly went out to the beach. He and his friends had driven down from Missouri for spring break. They were all students a Missouri State in Springfield, MO. At first he walked along the beautiful white sand shore line along the coast near Destin. They were staying in an inexpensive motel on the beach. He was enjoying watching the waves roll in and even the 5 or 6 dolphins swimming and jumping not too far out from the shore. The sun was peaking up with not a cloud in the sky. The temperature was about 70 and a beautiful morning.

Kevin was about to start jogging when he looked up and saw a cute girl approaching near him. She had shoulder length dark brown hair and the prettiest sky blue eyes he had ever seen. She had on very short shorts, t-shirt and tennis shoes.

As they approached each other, Kevin was looking her up and down. He said hello and she responded in a very soft voice and told him hello. She kept walking so Kevin went to jog down the beach. He figured he ran about 2 miles and stopped to catch his breath. Then he turned around and started jogging back. He met 3 or 4 other joggers on his journey back. When he got to the place where he had see the beautiful young lady earlier, there she was. He stopped and said "well hello again." Then she responded with her soft voice as she had done earlier except this time she didn't keep walking. He was very please about that.

Kevin told her his name and asked her for her name. She told him "my name is Terri." Being the gentleman he was he responded with "very nice to meet you Terri." Then she responded with the same.

"Well Terri where are you from?" She told him St. Louis and that she, her parents and a girl friend came down for a break from the city. He told her that he was from Springfield, Missouri and that he and his buddies were there for their spring break. "However my home town is Pella, Iowa."

She wanted to know what college he went to and he told her Missouri State. Then he asked her where she went to college. She said, "I don't, I'm a senior in high school. However I am considering going to Drury in Springfield next year."

Kevin was astonished and said, "oh wow, we will be in the same town and what a coincidence."

She asked if he and his friends drove down and said that she, her friend Sally, and her parents drove. He told her yes and there were 5 of them. They had borrowed his roommate Jake's mother's minivan so they would have more room. We are packed into this small room at the motel and his roommate from school had to sleep on the floor. Terri was very attentive while at the same time gazing out at the ocean. She spotted a couple of fishing boats and Kevin saw them too. Then she responded, "poor Jake having to sleep on the floor."

He probably didn't even realize it because the four of them got so drunk on beer and a few shots they were all crazy drunk. Kevin mentioned that he only had two beers because he was the designated driver. He also added that he was not much of a drinker and much preferred ice tea or a Coke. Kevin continued that they had arrived just before sunset the night before and his four buddies started drinking. At dark they loaded up in the van and went searching for a place to eat. He spotted a small seafood diner on the beach so they went in to eat. Two of his buddies said they sure hoped that this place served hamburgers. They lucked out because hamburgers were on the menu. The other three ordered the shrimp special and were glad they did because it was delicious. All five of us with fake I.D's in hand headed to the "Bikini Cove Bar" where all the waitresses wore bikinis. So we all ordered a beer and they were ordering a second one and he had hardly had a sip of his. A bunch of college girls walked in so they started mingling with them. Frank led the way because he was the best looking one of the bunch and they all followed, except for Kevin who stayed at the bar by himself. He walked out to the patio and wasn't in the mood to party. He was tired from the long trip down and was hoping to round up his buddies early and go to the motel to get some sleep. He drug his friends out of the bar at 1 a.m. and drove them back to the motel. They grabbed a cooler of beer and headed for the beach. Kevin went inside, stripped down to his boxers and crashed. His friends came stumbling in around four and he barely heard them. "I woke up around 6 and dressed and headed for the beach to jog and ran into you. So that's my story" he stated.

He then asked Terri, "did you and Sally go out last night?"

"No" she said. "We got here about dark, moved into the condo, freshened up a bit and went out to dinner with my parents. We went to a steak and seafood restaurant. My parents lean towards more fancy type restaurants. Dad has to have his scotch and mom her wine. After dinner they returned to the condo to sleep. Terri continued that she was the first one up, got dressed, woke up Sally and told her that she was going for a walk on the beach. Sally rolled over and went back to sleep. With that she stated, "and here I am." Kevin answered with, "I'm glad we ran into each other" Terri said, "me too."

CHAPTER 2

Kevin headed back to the motel and Terri walked the other direction towards her condo. He was mesmerized with how cute she was and her dark hair and blue eyes. He was hoping that he would see her again. All his friends were still asleep and poor Jake on the floor still wearing his clothes that he had on the night before. So he decided to take the van and go get something to eat. He found a McDonalds close by. He went through the drive-through and ordered his breakfast including three orange juices. He returned to the motel and ate his breakfast on the patio, and drank all three containers of orange juice. It got to be around 10:30 and Frank walked out in his boxers. He stretched and moaned trying to wake up. He said, "hey Kev, got any food left, I'm hungry." Kevin told him he had nothing left but McDonalds was close by if he wanted to take the van and get something to eat. Frank declined and went back in the room to wake the others up. Jake seemed to be in the worse shape so they stripped him down and threw him in the shower. The rest of them all showered, dressed, came to the patio, got the van keys and headed to McDonalds. While they were gone, Kevin showered, shaved, and put on his swim trunks, tank top, and flip flops and headed down to the beach.

An hour later the guys showed up in their swim trunks. Frank had on one of those new stretchy ones and was proud of his body as he should be because of his muscular lean physique. He shaved his chest, had some leg hair, no shirt on and a white towel around his neck and looked like a movie star. He headed straight to the ocean and went for a swim. Jake took off his shirt and had a weird tattoo on his chest that resembled a flying bird. The rest of the guys all made fun of it, but Jake was proud of it.

Kevin was a bit of a loner and not a big drinker like his buddies. They all had fun swimming and wrestling around in the water. Three cute girls came walking up and Frank hurried out of the water. Jake tried to make the first move but Frank told him to let him handle things. He sort of flexed his muscles and invited them to join them for a swim. Come to find out, they were college girls from Indiana and were also on their spring break.

After swimming for awhile the guys invited them up on the patio for a beer and the girls took them up on it. Kevin decided not to join them and went for a walk down the beach towards Terri's condo hoping to find her. Soon there she was under an umbrella with her girlfriend. He walked up and said, "well, fancy meeting you here." Terri introduced him to her friend Sally and acted like Kevin was a friend of hers.

"Hi Sally," he said with all his usual charm. "Why aren't you girls in the sun working on your Florida tans?"

Sally answered "are you kidding, with my red hair and fair skin I would burn to a crisp and get more freckles."

Terri said, "I like the sun and can probably tan in the shade."

They sat and visited for awhile and Kevin brought up the two fishing boats that he and Terri had seen that morning. He also mentioned that he would sure like to go out on one of them and try his luck fishing. "Why don't the three of us go out tomorrow" he announced.

Sally quickly responded, "are you kidding, I would really burn out there and I get sea sick. Terri's dad offered to take us and I quickly told him not me."

Kevin asked Terri if her dad liked to fish and she said yes he does. "Well then, maybe your dad, you and I could go out tomorrow. Do you think he would do that?"

"Probably, he really wants to do that," Terri answered. With that comment she was off to the condo to talk to her dad. Kevin was surprised with that and sat in Terri's chair and stated visiting with Sally. He did find out that they went to an all girls private high school, but that was about all he could get out of Sally.

CHAPTER 3

Terri went to the condo and her mom had just gotten back from the grocery store and asked Terri to put the groceries away. Terri told her that she would and she wanted to talk to dad about something. Her mom poured a cup of coffee and joined him on the deck and told him that Terri wanted to talk to him. She was about finished putting things away and her dad walked in to refill his coffee.

"Your mom said that you wanted to talk to me."

"Dad," she continued. "How about a fishing trip tomorrow, Sally and I met a guy today and he wants to go with us and he'll pay his share."

"What? a guy you met today and you want him to go with us?" her dad responded.

"Yes and I am sure you will like him and he has a manner about him you will admire."

"Okay, I will make the reservation and tell him to meet us at the pier at 7:00 and not to be late."

She leaned to her dad and gave him a kiss and a hug and thanked him dearly.

Terri took her dad to the beach to meet Kevin. Kevin jumped to his feet as soon as he saw them.

Terri said "Kevin, this is my father, James Carter."

Kevin immediately held out his hand and said, "Hello Mr. Carter, my name is Kevin Ruble and it is very nice to meet you." Kevin was very mannerly and extremely polite. This pleased Terri.

They visited for about ten minutes and Terri's dad said that he would book the fishing trip and told Kevin to be at the pier at seven sharp. Kevin told him he would be there early and wanted to pay his share. With that Mr. Carter said his goodbyes and told Kevin he would see him in the morning. Terri was all smiles.

Mr. Carter headed back to the condo, probably to tell his wife about Kevin and make the reservation for the fishing trip.

Terri said, "My dad is so cool and so considerate of things that I request of him." Sally responded, "He sure is, my dad would have marched right down here and told Kevin to get lost."

After they talked for a while, they decided to go for a swim, but not fair skinned Sally.

After swimming for a while Terri and Sally headed for the condo. Sally needed some air conditioning. Besides it was past time for lunch.

As they departed, Kevin told Terri that he would see her in the morning, and please thank her dad. He told her that he would pay his share tomorrow and Terri told him that her dad probably wouldn't let him.

With that they parted, Kevin heading for the motel and Terri and Sally for the condo.

CHAPTER 4

The girls walked into the condo for lunch, but instead Terri's mom started in on her. She knew that her dad had told her mom about Kevin and the fishing trip.

Mrs. Carter said, "Terri, are you crazy? You meet some beach bum college guy and invite him to go fishing with you and your dad."

"Mom, he is not a beach bum and you have this all wrong."

Before Mrs. Carter could speak, Sally spoke up, "I spent 30 minutes with him under the cabana and was very impressed with him. He is not only nice, but well mannered, and seems like a true gentleman. Maybe you should wait until you meet him before you pass judgment." Then she swallowed hard and hoped that Mrs. Carter hadn't taken offense to what she said.

After that Mrs. Carter turned silent and started putting out lunch. The girls and Terri's parents ate in silence until Terri's dad spoke up, "he seemed okay to me." Terri looked at her dad and grinned with satisfaction.

Her dad headed for the bedroom to take a nap and her mom poured a glass of wine and went out to the deck. Terri and Sally cleaned up the kitchen and did the dishes. Then they grabbed a coke and went out to the deck to join her mom. Terri spoke first, "mom, he is really a very nice person and a freshman at Mo. State in Springfield. I think you will like him when you meet him."

Mrs. Carter responded, "well, you are sure not going to Drury with that guy right across town."

"Come on mom, have an open mind and please don't make statements like this until you get to know him."

Mrs. Carter a little more mellow now said, "okay, we will see."

"Thanks mom and I love you." Sally gave her a thumbs up. They had a way of communicating without words.

Terri and Sally took a long walk on the beach. Sally with her 70 sunscreen and wearing a huge straw hat. Terri put on a 10 sunscreen and was already getting a tan. Sally only had about 100 more freckles that was her showcase for sunning.

Terri was hoping to run into Kevin, but didn't so they retreated to the condo for a nap. Mr. Carter was watching golf on T.V. and Mrs. Carter was in the huge hot tub on the deck. The girls went to their room. The sun and ocean had made them tired and sleepy.

Mrs. Clark woke them at 6:30 and told them to get ready to go to dinner. So the girls showered and did their hair and makeup. They dressed in cute sundresses and sandals and they were both ready in an hour.

Mr. Carter drove down the highway about 30 miles to a 5 star restaurant that he had found on the internet and had made an 8:30 reservation. The girls were glad that they had worn dresses because the place was very fancy. They were seated at a table by a window that had an ocean view. Terri knew that this dinner would be a 3 hour ordeal and lost all hope of seeing Kevin that night. Then she remembered the fishing trip at 7:00 A. M. and she would be spending all morning with him. Her parents had ordered a cocktail and the girls a coke. She and Sally ordered lobster, her dad a huge steak, and her mom stuffed crab. There were several courses and her dad had another scotch and her mom switched to wine. Everyone enjoyed all the courses and the girls raved over the lobster.

CHAPTER 5

Kevin spent the rest of the day with his buddies on the beach. There were several college kids around today and his buddies were all flirting with every girl they could. Kevin went to the snack shack and got an ice tea with lemon and retreated back to the patio and sat at the umbrella table to get some shade. He was watching all the people on the beach playing beach volleyball and throwing frisbees around. He wasn't in the mood to socialize. All he could think about was Terri and her beautiful hair and stunning eyes. About that time two guys walked by holding hands and carrying a small cooler and a canvas beach bag. Kevin could tell they had been in the sun to long and were turning a bright pink. He asked them if they wanted to join him under the umbrella and cool off a bit. It didn't bother him that they were gay, at least he thought they were. He was very open minded about the gay community. He never had any racial issues either. His best friend in high school was African American.

Kevin opened the conversation by asking them where they were from. They responded Michigan. They had flown to Florida and rented a car. They were roommates in college and were in their third year. They were staying at a high rise condo down the beach. While they talked, Kevin was thinking that they must be wealthy. They all three continued visiting and Kevin told them that he was from Iowa and went to college at Mo. State in Springfield, Mo. After a while they decided to head back to their condo and thanked Kevin for the shade. Kevin decided to go in for a nap and then take a shower and shave and get ready for dinner.

He napped about an hour and then as planned, he showered and shaved and dressed for dinner. When he was finished, he went down to the beach and told the guys he was getting hungry and they needed to decide where they were going for dinner. Some men were bringing in wood to build a bonfire and the guys wanted to hang around. Jake suggested they order pizza and the others agreed. Kevin volunteered to go get the pizzas and they all chipped in their money and asked him to also get a couple of cases of beer. All the kids were gathering around the bonfire and some had paired up. Frank of course had a beautiful, well endowed blond hanging on his arm.

Kevin went back to the room and called a nearby pizza place and ordered the pizzas. He found a grocery store and went inside and got two cases of beer and some chips and snacks. The lady asked for an I.D. so he showed her his fake I.D. and without question, checked him out. Kevin did not like going to liquor stores because they were very strict about I.D.s and that is why he chose a grocery store. Then he went to pick up the pizzas and headed back to the motel. He delivered the pizza and beer to the guys on the beach and they put the beer in the cooler and started gobbling down the pizza like they were starving to death. Luckily Kevin had collected enough money from them to pay for everything and he didn't have to contribute any of his. He took some pizza back up to the patio, got a beer, and sat at the table enjoying every bite. All he could think about was Terri and the fishing trip the next day.

Kevin went to bed early because he wanted to get up at 6 so that he could be at the pier before 7. He set his alarm on his cell phone before going to bed. He slept through the night hardly realizing when the guys came in. When the alarm went off he immediately sprang out of bed and noticed that Jake was in Frank's bed and figured that Frank had got lucky and went home with the blond.

Kevin dressed in shorts, tennis shoes, and a nice t-shirt from Mo. State. He rolled his sun screen in his beach towel, grabbed his phone, and took off for the lobby. He asked the clerk if there was a cab company that he could call. The clerk told him that the motel had a shuttle and would be glad to drive him. Kevin told him the name of the pier and he said that it was only about three miles from there. The shuttle had just pulled up and a bunch of drunken kids were staggering out.

The driver of the shuttle appeared to be about 18 or so. The clerk asked him to take Kevin to the pier. He told Kevin to sit up front because he hadn't cleaned out the back and no telling what he would find when he did.

Kevin said okay and jumped in the front seat. They were at the pier in about 10 minutes. Kevin tipped him $5 and headed down the pier. It was 6:45 and Terri and her dad had not arrived yet. In 10 minutes, he looked up and saw them starting down the pier. Terri looked so cute in short cut offs, t-shirt, and tennis shoes. Her dad looked like he was going on an African Safari. He had kaki shorts, shirt, and hat on and even his socks were kaki colored.

Mr. Carter had rented the most expensive boat. There were only two couples on the boat beside the 3 of them. There was a small breakfast bar and a full bar and bartender down below.

Mr. Carter said, "how about a Bloody Mary to start off our day." Terri responded, "I may not like it dad." He answered "then I'll drink yours." Mr. Carter ordered the drinks, the bartender mixed them up, and handed them all their Bloody Marys, and no I.D. required. Kevin was glad because he didn't want Mr. Carter to know that he had a fake one.

They headed up to the main deck and the helpers were getting the gear ready for the morning. They sat down and started drinking their cocktails. Kevin thought to himself that this was probably only the second Bloody Mary he had ever drunk, but never this early in the morning, and especially before breakfast. He thought it tasted pretty good but when he looked at Terri she was making a weird face. He could tell that she wasn't too fond of it. Kevin gave her a smile and she grinned back and handed her drink to her dad.

Terri told her dad that she was hungry and wanted to go eat. Mr. Carter told her that she and Kevin could go ahead and he would be down in a bit. They both enjoyed a breakfast of scrambled eggs, bacon, and toast with jelly. Terri ordered hot tea but Kevin still had half of his Bloody Mary to finish. They sat at a table near a small port hole and enjoyed their breakfast and their time being together alone.

As they finished, Mr. Carter came down and announced that the boat was about to launch. He grabbed a bacon and egg sandwich and the three of them headed up on deck. They took their places. The workers came over and told them about fishing. Then they were in the bay and headed to the ocean. The water was very calm and the waves were small.

The bartender showed up to take drink orders. Mr. Carter ordered coffee, Terri a coke, and Kevin ice tea with lemon. He was back in a few minutes and they were headed out to sea.

This was not a deep sea fishing boat. They were going to bottom fish. In about 20 minutes the boat came to a stop and they were instructed what to do. They were each given a pole with 5 hooks on it and live bait. The bottom one was baited with something that looked like raw liver. Kevin told Terri that he had never done this before and was very excited. It was also a first for Terri and her dad.

They were instructed to drop their lines and let them sink to the bottom. The water was about 40 feet deep and they were told to be patient until the fish could smell that liver, and when they felt a few good tugs on their lines to reel it in. They could catch 3 or 4 fish at a time.

After about 15 minutes one of the other guys pulled up his line and had 2 small red snappers. The worker took them off and threw them back telling them they were too small to keep. Then the captain started the engine and they were instructed to reel in their lines. He drove farther down the coast and a little farther out in the ocean. When he stopped they were instructed to drop their lines. The water was about 60 feet deep. In just a few minutes, Kevin felt a couple of tugs and reeled it in. He had 3 good size red snapper and was so excited about what he had done. Terri just looked at him and smiled.

Then Terri's line tugged and she reeled it in but only had one huge fish on it. The worker said it was a grouper and it was unusual to catch one there because they are usually farther out to sea. He told her she was a lucky gal as he rebated both Terri's and Kevin's lines. They dropped them back in and Terri's dad started reeling in. He had 4 really good size red snapper and was thrilled. He had Terri take a picture of him and his first catch. The other couples were reeling in and catching 3 or 4 themselves.

After a couple hours, the captain said it was time to go in. They all reeled up their lines and both Terri and Kevin had fish on them. Kevin had a huge red snapper and one good size sea bass. Terri had 3 red snapper on hers and all keepers. All the fish were put in live wells and the workers collected everyone's poles and put them away. Before the boat took off the bartender showed up. Mr. Carter ordered coffee, and the kids declined.

Kevin was hot and pulled off his shirt and then got his sunscreen and started spraying himself. Terri noticed that he did not shave his chest and had just the right amount of hair to make him look manly and sexy, at least in her opinion. Then she offered to spray his back. She pulled off her shirt and was wearing a bright red bikini top and asked Kevin to spray her. So he did her back and she faced him so he sprayed her chest and stomach too. Mr. Carter was getting a kick out of them while sipping his coffee. He asked to borrow the spray for his knees that were already getting red.

The captain headed back towards the pier. Kevin figured it would take 20 minutes or so and asked Terri if she wanted to walk around. She definitely did because she was tired of sitting. Kevin's intention was to be alone with her away from her dad. They walked behind the engine room where the captain was driving and stopped in the shade. They were standing and holding on to the rail when all of a sudden, they hit a big wave and the boat really rocked. Terri lost her balance and started to stumble and Kevin caught her. He pulled her close, their eyes met, and without thinking, he kissed her. Kevin started to apologize and Terri stopped him, told him she liked it and also liked his hairy chest. Kevin laughed and they both hung to the rail in case they hit another wave.

Soon they were at the pier and the workers were tying up the boat. They walked to where her dad was and he was gathering up their stuff getting ready to get on the pier. The workers were bringing the fish to the deck so they all could pick out what they wanted to take with them. Mr. Carter told them that he wanted the grouper and also some red snapper. Kevin said, "how about my sea bass?" So Mr. Carter told them to throw in some of the bass.

Terri asked her dad what he was going to do with all that fish. He told her that he was going to cook it. She didn't even know he knew how to cook fish.

They walked back to where their SUV was parked. Mr. Carter asked Kevin where his car was and he told him that he was going to call the motel to have them send a shuttle. Mr. Carter replied, "nonsense, hop in with us and we will drop you off. He rode in back and Terri up front with her dad. When Kevin told Mr. Carter he wanted to pay for his share of the fishing trip, Mr. Carter again told him, "nonsense." Mr. Carter had put it on his credit card and tipped all the attendants $20. Kevin figured it was probably $800 or more. When they got to the motel, Kevin was getting out and saying his thanks, Mr. Carter spoke up and invited him to dinner at the condo. Kevin was surprised and accepted the invitation immediately. He was told to be there by 7:00.

After they dropped Kevin off Mr. Carter headed for the grocery store to get some items for dinner and seasoning for the fish. He got everything for Terri's mom to make Ceasar salad and twice baked potatoes.

When they got back to the condo and took in the groceries and that huge plastic bag of cleaned fish, he started bragging to his wife and Sally what great fishermen they were, and especially Terri because she caught the only grouper. Then he held up the bag of fish and announced that he was cooking fish for dinner that night. He politely asked his wife if she would make the Ceasar salad and the twice baked potatoes and that he had bought all the ingredients that she would need. He put the fish in the refrigerator and asked Terri to put away the rest of the groceries. As he was headed for their bedroom to wash up and change clothes he turned and told his wife to make enough salad for 5 because he had invited Kevin. With that he walked away before his wife could respond.

Mrs. Carter looked at Terri suspiciously. Terri told her it was totally all dad's idea. Then she stated, "I didn't know dad knew how to cook fish."

CHAPTER 6

About four o'clock that afternoon Terri talked Sally into going to the beach for a swim.

Terri was hoping to see Kevin but he was in his motel room trying to figure out what to wear for dinner. Sally finally stated that there was no Kevin on the beach and begged Terri to go to the pool where there was more shade and so Terri agreed.

Sally dove right in the deep end and Terri followed. They were having fun together as usual. Soon they were on a pool chair with a cool icy coke. The conversation led to Kevin. Terri told Sally that he had kissed her that morning and she loved it. Sally said, "Lucky, I'm jealous". "Don't be" said Terri. "This could go nowhere but I'm hoping for the best. I have never met such a good looking, non-conceited and considerate guy, ever!" Sally sighed with envy.

About six that evening they headed up to the condo to shower and clean up. They found her dad in the kitchen getting ready to start seasoning the fish. There was so much fish. He was planning to fry and even bake some. He poured a scotch and a glass of wine and delivered it to his wife on the deck. He asked her sweetly if she would please come make the Caesar dressing. She responded she would and then he knew how to get to her by serving her wine. She asked him to go see if the condo had a blender and of course it did.

Mrs. Carter finally came wandering into the kitchen and started on the dressing. When it was done she got the Romaine lettuce out and washed it and then started patting it dry with paper towels. As she was doing this she asked her husband why he had invited this Kevin guy to dinner. She was still reluctant. She put some large salad plates into the freezer to chill. Mr. Carter said "wait until you get to know him better. He is very smart, extremely polite, mannerly and he seems to think and also treat our daughter very special. Just give him a chance". She grew silent.

About that time Sally showed up in cute shorts, flip flops with jewelry on them and a tank top showing off her new found freckles. Mrs. Carter asked her to set the table on the deck for dinner. Sally collected the plates, silverware and napkins and headed up to the deck. Then she found a couple of candles in the living room and took them out to the table and carefully placed them in just the right spot. She returned asking Mrs. Carter what glasses to put on the table and Mrs. Carter said to wait.

Terri was still in the bedroom primping for the evening and decided to wear the cute sundress she had worn the night before and put on some cute sandals with straps around the ankles. She finally appeared in the kitchen and her mom noticed a little more make-up on her and her hair had been curled. This was unusual for Terri. Her dad complimented her but her mom just stared.

At the last minute Mr. Carter decided to grill the fish instead of bake it. He asked Terri and Sally to start the gas grill. The grill looked brand new and had an automatic starter so the job was easy to do. Pretty soon her dad came out and covered the whole grill with foil he had sprayed so the fish would not stick. Then he went back to the kitchen to check on the baked potatoes. He scrubbed the potatoes and smeared them with butter and covered them in sea salt and wrapped them loosely in foil. They were baking away. He decided not to have them twice baked.

Well at 7pm the doorbell rang. Terri ran to answer it and of course it was Kevin. He looked really sharp in his shorts, polo shirt and sandals. The shirt looked a bit large on him but Terri could care less. He was carrying a bouquet of flowers for Mrs. Carter.

Kevin had decided to borrow one of Frank's polos. It was wrinkled so he hung it next to the shower hoping that the steam from the shower would take some of the wrinkles out. When he got out of the shower he took his hands and smoothed the wrinkles out the best he could. Then he shaved, brushed his teeth and styled his hair with a bit of Jake's hair gel. He looked at his fingernails and decided to trim them a bit. Since he was wearing sandals he checked out his toenails and decided to trim them too. His feet looked dry, probably from the salt water and sand. So he went digging through Frank's bag and found some lotion and applied it to his feet. Only Frank, out of the five of them, would have lotion. And Kevin knew that. So now he felt ready for the dinner with Terri and her parents and of course Sally. He decided to walk the road instead of the beach so his feet would not be covered with sand. It would take ten minutes longer but he had the time. He had bought the flowers at a quick stop on his way.

Terri showed him in smiling the whole time and so was he. They both had beautiful perfect teeth and it was very noticeable when they smiled.

Terri first took Kevin in the kitchen to say hi to her dad. He was heating up the skillet to fry the fish he had breaded. The salad and dressing were in the refrigerator ready to be tossed and the potatoes were baking.

Mrs. Carter reached out and welcomed Kevin with a generous handshake and Kevin politely thanked them for inviting him to dinner. Mr. Carter offered Kevin a beer or a cocktail. Kevin responded with "that Bloody Mary I had this morning is plenty for me in one day". Mrs. Carter was pleased with the answer and Kevin asked if they might have iced tea or he would have a coke. Mr. Carter said they have iced tea and lemon wedges in the refrigerator and to help himself. So Terri got three glasses and gave one to Kevin for the tea and poured coke in the other two for her and Sally.

Terri said, "lets go out to the deck and take Sally her coke and see what she and my mom are up too." Kevin followed her to the deck, held out his hand to shake hands with Mrs. Carter and reluctantly she held out her hand and welcomed him. Sally and Terri grinned at each other. Kevin gave Mrs. Carter the flowers and she thanked him and smiled.

After about ten minutes Mr. Carter showed up with a tray of seasoned fish and put It all on the grill. He closed the lid and handed Kevin the barbeque utensils. He asked Kevin if he knew how to grill. Kevin said he was pretty good at steaks and burgers but had never grilled fish. Mr. Carter told him the grill was in his hands because he would be busy in the kitchen. He told Kevin to wait ten minutes, check it, flip it over and wait another five minutes. Mr. Carter had seasoned it with lemon pepper, mint and lemon juice. He walked away instructing Kevin not to burn it. Kevin did not have a watch on so he set his cell phone alarm for eight minutes. Poor Kevin was so nervous he could not even visit with the ladies. Terri patted his arm and told him not to worry that he would do fine. She went back into the kitchen to get her mom some more wine. When she returned she told her mom that her dad needed her in the kitchen to toss the salad and get the potatoes out of the oven to rest before opening the foil. So Mrs. Carter headed for the kitchen. Kevin's phone alarm went off so he looked at the fish and decided to flip it over. Sally and Terri agreed. He set the alarm for five more minutes.

In a few minutes Mrs. Carter showed up with the chilled plates and the salad. Mr. Carter took the fried fish out of the pans; put it on a rack in the upper oven at a very low temperature to keep it warm and placed the potatoes next to the rack. He grabbed his second scotch and his wife's wine bottle as Kevin was removing the fish from the grill and putting it on a baking tray. Mr. Carter put it in the oven with the other fish and returned to the deck and complimented Kevin on how well the grilled fish was cooked. And of course Kevin thanked him. Mrs. Carter started dishing up the salad and served it with some nice garlic bread that Mr. Carter had prepared.

The salad tasted excellent to Kevin. He had only had Caesar salad a couple of times. His mom never made it at home. He told Mrs. Carter that was the very best Caesar salad he had ever eaten and thanked her for making it. With that, Terri looked at him, winked and smiled.

When they completed eating the salad Sally stood up and removed the salad plates and headed for the kitchen. Mr. Carter had the fish and potatoes (including the toppings on the counter) and asked Sally to go get the rest to come to the kitchen and fill their plates. So everyone came to the kitchen and Kevin insisted all the ladies go before him. Mr. Carter however insisted that Kevin go before him. Everyone took some grilled and fried fish. Mr. Carter pointed out what was the grouper. Kevin made sure he chose that because Terri had caught it. He also chose some sea bass that he caught.

They all doctored up their baked potatoes and headed for the deck just in time to watch the beautiful sunset. The sky was orange and yellow over the ocean and the sun was just about to sink into the water.

Then Sally quickly lit the candles and they began to eat. Mr. Carter kept complimenting Kevin on the grilled fish. Kevin finally said "thank you but Mr. Carter you did the hard part which was the seasoning." Mr. Carter responded and asked Kevin to call him Ron and his wife Judy. Kevin replied that he would try and Terri kept grinning like a twelve year old even though she was seventeen.

Sally and Terri started clearing the table and Kevin offered to help but Terri told him no and to sit there, relax and visit with her parents. As she exited with both hands full of dishes she glanced back to see if Kevin was alright with that and he seemed to be doing okay.

The first thing out of Mrs. Carters mouth was "well Kevin, where did you grow up?" Kevin answered "In a small Dutch settlement about thirty miles south of Des Moines, Iowa. The name of the town is Pella." Mrs. Carter quickly responded "A group of people from our church took a trip there by bus for some kind of festival last spring." Kevin quicky answered "Yes, that is our tulip festival. Every street is lined with tulips and the town square has a huge windmill with a bandstand and bleachers to watch all the performers." "Oh yes," said Mrs. Carter. "Tell me more about the town, your upbringing and your parents." Kevin being very polite told her his parents are not from Dutch descent but moved there from Des Moines before he was born. His dad owned a construction company and his mother had a gift and craft shop on the square. She sold handmade things from Dutch ladies in the area. Her business was exploding until they built an interstate that by passed the town and her business fell by fifty percent in one year. But dad keeps busy building pole barns and a few new houses now and then so they make enough for me to go to college and take care of my younger sister.

Mrs. Carter started asking some personal questions but Kevin didn't mind. He told her his younger sister was eight years younger; a cute girl with tons of personality, a great soccer player and is learning to play the trumpet and piano. Her name is Cat, that's short for Catherine which is our grandma's name. He also included that when he is home he works sometimes in construction for his dad and sometimes in his moms' store helping with displays or painting a wall or two.

Mrs. Carter seemed pleased with Kevin's answers and retreated to the kitchen to see how the girls were doing. Mr. Carter told Kevin not to be upset with his wife. She was just curious about his background. Kevin told him that he didn't mind at all and he understood her concerns.

CHAPTER 7

Mr. Carter was yawning and was starting to act very tired. Mrs. Carter and the girls returned and Mr. Carter stated he was ready for bed and Mrs. Carter joined him. Sally said, "it is about eleven and I'm going to bed too."

Terri and Kevin headed for the beach. Kevin sat down in a beach lounge chair and to his surprise Terri sat in his lap. She came toward his face with hers and he kissed her madly like a groom would kiss his bride when a minister would announce "you can now kiss the bride". After that, she sat up in Kevin's lap and said "let's talk". Kevin agreed and they started up a serious conversation.

She asked Kevin if he thought they would see each other in college if she went to Drury. Or if her dad won and she went to Washington University would he come to visit her in St. Louis. Kevin immediately said yes to both situations. He was actually having very strong feelings for her and he had only kissed her twice. Terri was pleased with that answer and announced the serious talk was over. She leaned in toward Kevin and kissed him again. They made out on the beach recliner for awhile but Kevin, being the gentleman that he was, kept his hands to himself.

It was about midnight and Terri said she had better go in before her mother came looking for her. As she started for the condo Kevin asked "Can I see you tomorrow?" Terri answered "Right here at 8 am" and turned to go inside.

Kevin started his walk back to the motel almost singing with delight. He passed some kids at a bonfire. They asked him to join but he declined. He got back to the room and his buddies were gone and so was the van. He figured they were at the bars. He cleared the clothes and damp towels off the bed, stripped down to his boxers and crashed.

He barely woke up at 4:30 when his buddies came in. He told them to quiet down and go to bed. In a few minutes he heard one of them in the bathroom. He looked around and everyone was in their place except Jake. Kevin rolled over and fell back to sleep.

He was awake at 7:30 and had just enough time to get ready to meet Terri. He pulled on his swim trunks, found a tank top, flip flops and went into the bathroom. It was disgusting. He took a pee, brushed his teeth and splashed some water on his face. He picked up his hair brush, wet his hair down, brushed it and out the door he went.

He had time so he went to the lobby to ask if the maids could go to their room and clean the bathroom and leave some fresh towels. He warned the clerk what the bathroom looked like and apologized. The clerk told him the maids would not be there until 10 but they would get to it after lunch sometime. So Kevin reassured him he would have his friends up and out of there by 12:30 and thanked the clerk.

It was 7:45 by then so he took off his flip flops and jogged to meet Terri so he would not be late. He arrived at 7:59 but Terri wasn't there yet. So he sat in the same lounge chair and started watching the dolphins swimming and jumping out of the water. The gulf was so calm that morning. Hardly a wave was hitting the beach.

About 8:10 Terri snuck up on him and he about jumped out of his shirt. He started laughing and sprang to his feet, pulled her close and kissed her. Then he said "good morning". She giggled and then replied "good morning to you too". They sat in regular chairs holding hands, talking and watching the dolphins performing for them. It was a great morning.

After about an hour he mentioned he would like to go get some juice or maybe a snack. She offered to go to the condo and get him some but he had a better idea. "Let's walk down to the snack shack and get something. They open at nine and it's about quarter after." She agreed and they began walking on the shoreline looking for seashells along the way. There were only little tiny ones because the water was too calm to wash up any bigger ones.

They arrived at the snack shack. He told Terri to order first. She couldn't decide what she wanted and told him to go ahead. He ordered an egg and bacon sandwich on toast and a large orange juice. She told them that she would have the same but a medium juice. The food was ready in about ten minutes. Kevin pulled out a twenty dollar bill from his swimsuit pocket and paid the bill. There was a small eating area there with a few tables with umbrellas. They sat down and Kevin offered to put up the umbrella. She declined and said it was not necessary.

By then the beach was beginning to fill up with quite a few people; Some walking, some jogging and some with a bad hangover just sitting in the sand and holding their heads. They were probably thinking to themselves "why the hell did I drink so much last night?" Kevin knew that when some of his buddies woke up they would be thinking the same thing, especially Jake. However, Frank would probably get up and stir the others. He always seem to hold his liquor like a pro.

A few more people came to the snack shack; some just for coffee and others for breakfast. By then Kevin and Terri were finished. They cleared their table off and threw the trash in the large can beside the shack.

They walked slowly back to her condo. She wanted to be close by in case her parents came looking for her. The dolphins were gone by now and some people were taking a morning swim. They grabbed the cabana her father had reserved so when the sun got hot they would have some protection.

About that time Sally came out to join them. She was already covered in lotion along with her cover up and one of Mrs. Carter's straw hats. Actually she looked very fashionable except for her big pink framed sunglasses. Terri started laughing and stated that those were her mom's hat and crazy sunglasses. Sally told them that Terri's mom was the one who put the SPF70 lotion all over her. Terri gave Sally her spot in the shade and moved around by Kevin putting her beach towel in the sand. After twenty minutes or so she reached in her bag and got out her SPF15 lotion. She applied it to her face, arms, legs, feet and chest. She asked Kevin to apply some to her back. As he started he saw Mrs. Carter about ten feet away watching but trying not to be obvious. Kevin jumped up and greeted her kindly and offered her the lounge chair in the shade. She thanked him.

Terri said "Kevin aren't you going to finish my back?" Still holding the bottle he glanced at Terri's mom as if waiting for her permission and then continued what he was doing.

Mrs. Carter drilled Kevin for awhile about college. How did he like it, did he make good grades and what was his major? He told her he really liked Missouri State but was staying in a freshman dorm, the oldest one on campus and was anxious to move into a nicer one his sophomore year. He told her he had a 3.7 GPA his first semester but was planning on bringing it up that semester. He explained his major was math but he was strongly considering changing it to mathematical engineering. He told her there were only about twenty students with that major and that his advisor had recommended he switch to it. So he has seriously been thinking about it. She told him he will have to explain it more sometime but right now she was going for a swim.

She stood up took off her cover up and big hat but left her big framed sunglasses on. Kevin noticed the sunglasses matched her blue and green one piece swimsuit. He hadn't noticed the night before probably because he was so nervous. She had a nice figure, about 5'6", slender and what he thought to be a salon color of blonde. It was cut short with lots of fringe around the face. He must have not even looked at her hair the night before.

She headed for the ocean and Sally decided to accompany her. They were in the water about fifteen minutes both agreeing how nice and warm the water felt. They patted themselves dry and returned to the lounge chairs in the shade. Kevin and Terri stayed in the sun sharing a towel.

About that time a cocktail waitress from the condo bar at the pool arrived. She wanted to know if they would like something to drink. Mrs. Carter ordered lemonades, the two girls a coke and Kevin his usual ice tea with lemon. When she brought the drinks, Mrs. Carter added a generous tip and signed the check. Kevin only had four dollars left from his breakfast and offered it to pay for his tea. Mrs. Carter told him that was not necessary and to put his money away. She stated that her husband would pay when they checked out in the morning. Kevin was very surprised to hear her say that. Terri hadn't said a word about it. He decided he would talk to Terri about it later.

CHAPTER 8

Mrs. Carter stood up and announced that she was going back to the condo. She said she wanted to shower and do her hair before her husband came back. Mr. Carter was playing golf at some swanky club somewhere on the gulf. Sally announced she was going to stay awhile longer. As Mrs. Carter headed for the condo, Terri got up and jumped in the chair and motioned for Kevin to sit with her and get out of the sun for awhile. Kevin had really started to develop a good tan but took her up on the offer so they could talk. He knew he could discuss the matter at present in front of Sally. Besides, Sally looked like she was falling asleep with a nice gentle ocean breeze blowing in on her.

Kevin began the conversation after rubbing his tearful eyes "Terri, you didn't tell me you had to leave tomorrow. This is our last afternoon and evening to see each other." Terri responded "I know it's the pits but dad has to get back for a big meeting at the University. The meeting is Friday and tomorrow is Thursday so we have to leave." Kevin got a little teary eyed again but tried to look away so Terri wouldn't notice. But she did.

She gave him a big hug and a kiss on the cheek and said "I am so sorry; I don't want to leave with you here."

Kevin replied "We have to work something out so we can be together this afternoon and tonight." He asked her for her cell phone number but she said her parents wouldn't let her have one until she went to college. So he wrote his number down and gave it to her. She immediately put it in a change purse in her bag.

Kevin was worried about his buddies not being out of the room so he asked Terri to walk back with him and told her why. When they arrived at the motel, his buddies were all gone except for Jake. He was on the patio drinking a bottle of water trying to sober up and get over his hangover.

Kevin saw two maids with a cart heading their way. It was about one o'clock. The maids asked if the room was vacant and he said yes. He followed them in the and told them if they would just clean the bathroom and leave fresh towels that would be enough. One of the maids said "No, we are putting on clean sheets and vacuuming too. So get busy and pick up all those clothes and put them in the closet. We will get busy cleaning in the bathroom first". He knew better than to argue with them. So he went out on the patio to fetch Jake to help but he was in no shape to help. Terri told Kevin she would help but he refused saying "You're not seeing this mess". So he went back inside starting to throw clothes in the closet floor and extra towels on the floor by the bathroom. Then he piled everyone's duffle bags on top of the dirty stinky clothes in the bottom of the closet. Being the person that he is, he even stripped the beds for the maids and threw them on the pile with the dirty towels.

He then went outside and a got a clean wash cloth off the maids cart, dunked it in the cooler of cold water and gave it to Jake. Jake actually said thanks and applied it to his head. He went back in to find his duffle bag and got his last forty dollars and gave the maids twenty of it and thanked them dearly.

He went back outside and told Terri he wanted to go somewhere. First he stopped in the lobby and asked the clerk where an ATM machine could be found. The clerk told him there was one about two blocks west of there. He and Terri walked down there. He had twenty dollars and his debit card. He withdrew two hundred dollars from the ATM and then spotted a café on the second floor in a small shopping center. He told Terri he wanted to have dinner there so they could talk. She agreed and they headed for the café. The place only had about ten or twelve tables but there was a table for two by the window with a great view of the beach. They both ate a light lunch of shrimp salad over spinach leaves and breadsticks.

Kevin started speaking first and asked Terri about going to Drury. She said her mom wanted her to go because her mom's sister had graduated from there and was all for Terri going there. But Terri also included that her dad was arguing for Washington University because her tuition would practically be nothing due to his position and then she could live at home. She also told Kevin that she had already been accepted at both colleges. Her mom had even sent in a deposit for a dorm that her aunt recommended at Drury.

Kevin in turn remarked that he was in favor of Drury but if it didn't happen he would be making some trips to St. Louis. She smiled and told Kevin that made her happy and she wants to see him as often as they could work it out.

CHAPTER 9

It was now going on 3 o'clock. They walked to the beach and headed in the direction of Terri's condo. They were walking very slowly and once in awhile waded in the ocean waves trying to splash one another. When they returned to the condo they sat in the cabana and were talking about how to persuade her dad into letting her go to Drury.

The cocktail waitress came by and they ordered their usual. When the waitress brought the drinks, Kevin was digging in his pocket for cash while Terri grabbed the check, signed it and included a five dollar tip. Kevin said, "This is on me". Terri responded, "Too late, you bought lunch so it's my turn." He leaned over and gave her a quick kiss and said "Thank you, you sneaky lady". Terri started laughing.

Then out of the clear blue, Terri shocked him by saying "Have you ever had sex?" He sat there almost stunned that she wanted to know this so early in their relationship. She said "Now be honest. I will not be offended if you have." He then told her that he had two times; once his senior year in high school and the other last fall at college. "Were you dating these girls at the time?" Terri wanted to know. He said "Actually, no". Kevin quickly tried to change the subject but Terri was being persistent. "Tell me more. Where did it take place?" So being put on the spot, Kevin decided to be honest. After all, wasn't honesty supposed to be a big part of relationships?

He explained that in high school it was his second date with this girl. They went to a party at a farm and the party was outside. The owner of the property didn't live there. He just used it for growing corn and soybeans. His grandson was throwing the party and he was a junior at my school. Kevin and his date had four or five beers and she told him she wanted to go somewhere private. So they took his Jeep and drove out to a small lake at the edge of town. He pulled up in a spot facing the lake and before he could turn the car lights out, she pulled off her t-shirt with no bra on and her breasts fully exposed. He turned out the lights and they started making out. The next thing he knew they were in the back of the Jeep both naked. She had given Kevin a rubber for protection and no baby. They quickly did it, both satisfied. They got dressed and drove back to town. He pulled up in her drive. She leaned over and kissed him and told him she had a great time and got out of the car. He drove home, quietly got into bed and thought to himself "what just happened?" Too much alcohol is what just happened. When he woke up the next morning he felt hung over and very guilty for having sex with her. Most guys would have been bragging to everyone but Kevin never told a sole until now when he was telling Terri. He also said that the girl's dad got transferred to another state so her family moved and he only saw her at school a few times before they moved.

"Okay, now tell me about the second time" begged Terri. He told her that he was on a blind date and they went to a party at a fraternity house. Lots of beer and booze was being consumed and loud, loud music playing. He noticed a few couples heading upstairs. His date wanted to get the hell out of there. They walked across campus to his dorm and he invited her up to his room. His roommate Jake had gone home for the weekend. As soon as they walked in the room she pulled Kevin's shirt off and started unbuttoning his jeans. She pulled them down to expose an erect penis. She proceeded to give him oral sex. When he had ejaculated she kissed him goodnight and left, leaving Kevin standing there with his jeans around his ankles and his shoes on. He was so stunned at what had just happened and still feeling very drunk he undressed, took a hot shower and went to bed. He never saw the girl again. She had dropped out of school and left town. That's when Kevin really slowed down on his drinking.

"So there Terri, now you know. Now tell me about your sexual encounters" he stated with an embarrassed voice. She laughed and said "you're kidding, I go to an all girls school and have dated very little and I am a virgin."

Kevin didn't know what to say so they sat there in silence sipping on their drinks. About that time Sally walked up and wanted to know where they had been. She had been looking for them earlier because Mrs. Carter wanted to take them shopping. So Sally and Mrs. Carter went shopping without Terri. Sally told Terri she better go up to the condo and check in with her mom because she was a little worrie

So Terri headed to the condo and Sally joined Kevin under the cabana. Sally wanted to know where they had been. Kevin told her about the finding the small café and having lunch. Then he mentioned they had gone for a long walk on the beach and splashed around in the waves. Sally told him that the relationship between him and Terri looked like something special was developing and Kevin's response was "I sure hope so."

Mrs. Carter seemed relieved to see Terri. She told her she missed out on the shopping trip but she had bought her something and it was on her bed. Terri went to see what it was and her mom followed. It was the cutest pair of designer jeans and a great looking blouse with a tank top to wear under it. There was also the cutest pair of sandals she had ever seen. She gave her mom a big hug and thanked her. Her mom said her dad had called and said to get a cab and come to the country club for dinner at 6:30. He had made a reservation. Terri asked her mom cautiously if Kevin could go. Her mom replied she guessed so because her dad had made the reservation for five and wanted Kevin to join them.

Terri was elated and ran back to the beach to tell Kevin and Sally about dinner. At first Kevin said "I can't do that, your parents have already spent too much money on me and I feel awkward about it". Terri answered him, "Don't be silly. They can afford it and besides Dad told mom to bring you and he had made the reservation for five at 6:30 p.m."

Kevin really didn't know what to do. He didn't want Terri's parents to think he was trying to take advantage of them. Terri begged him some more and he finally said he would go. Terri said "it is 4:30 and we are getting a cab at 6. I need to go shower and wash my hair". Kevin replied "I need a shower and shave myself but what should I wear?" Terri said "Casual, shorts or whatever. I am sure my dad has shorts and some kind of golf shirt on and a visor up on his head."

Kevin stood up, gave Terri a quick kiss and said "I'll go clean up and be back to your condo before six". He then proceeded to walk the beach back to the motel. When he walked into the room he was surprised to see it clean with the beds made and a sparkling clean bathroom. He opened the closet door to get his duffle bag and saw everything piled in the floor that he had put there earlier. He grabbed his one and only pair of jeans he brought and had hung in the closet, grabbed a pair of underwear and headed into the bathroom to shower and shave. When he was done he put on jeans and went out and found his sandals under the bed and was digging for a shirt to wear. He had pretty much worn all his nicer shirts so he went searching through Franks' things and found the other clean polo he had brought and decided to wear it. It was somewhat wrinkled but he didn't have time to steam it in the shower. He put it on, went in the bathroom and tried to smooth out the front of the shirt with his hand and heat from the motel hair dryer. It seemed to help so he sprayed on his cologne, brushed his damp hair again and was ready to go. It was quarter to six so he had to get going because he was taking the road. It was the long way to the condo because he didn't want his feet and sandals to be covered with sand.

He arrived at the condo shortly before six. Terri answered the door and looked beautiful. She told him she was wearing the outfit her mom had bought her that day. With that Mrs. Carter came out and said the cab should be waiting. Terri hollered for Sally and they all headed out the door. The cab was waiting and the three ladies sat in the back and Kevin sat up front with the driver.

When they arrived at the club, the driver said forty dollars. Kevin quickly handed him fifty dollars and told him to keep the change. Mrs. Carter was astonished that Kevin had beat her to pay for the cab. She said "You shouldn't have done that because you are our guest". He then told her "It was my pleasure".

Dinner went well with really good food. Mr. Carter ordered steak and insisted on Kevin to order steak too. Kevin couldn't remember the last time he had steak. His mouth was already watering for it after Mr. Carter's suggestion. He ordered a twelve ounce sirloin. Mr. Carter told the waiter to make it the sixteen ounce.

CHAPTER 10

After dinner Mr. Carter ordered him and his wife coffee and a brandy. He asked the kids if they wanted another coke or something. Terri thanked him and told her parents they were going outside to the patio to come and get them when they were ready to go. As they entered the patio it was obvious there was nowhere to sit so they just walked around. Forty-five minutes had passed and Terri saw her dad at the railing of the patio. He spotted them and motioned for them to come. They met her parents in front of the club and Mr. Carter had already summoned the valet for his car. As the car arrived, the valet opened the doors and politely helped Mrs. Carter into the front seat. Then he ran around and closed the door for Mr. Carter. The kids were already in the back and had closed their own door. Mr. Carter sat in the driver's seat for a few seconds, turned around and told Terri she had better drive because he had been drinking. So he got out and Kevin let Terri out. Sally moved to the middle and Mr. Carter sat behind Terri. The valet closed the door for Terri and they headed home. Not much conversation took place on the way back; mostly small talk about how great the dinner was.

Once they arrived at the condo Mr. Carter just sat in his seat. So Terri opened his door, put a hand on his shoulder and told him to come on. He snorted and got out of the car. Terri joked with him and said "Am I going to have to put you to bed too"? Everyone laughed. Kevin shook Mr. Carter's hand and dearly thanked him for dinner and a great evening. He turned to thank Mrs. Carter and he leaned toward her and she gave him a slight hug and whispered not to keep her out too late because they were leaving at six in the morning. Kevin smiled at her and said "Okay, I won't, promise".

Mr. and Mrs. Carter headed for the condo and Sally decided to go with them to pack and get some sleep before the long trip home the next day.

Kevin and Terri headed for the beach. It was a warm evening and only a bit of a breeze now and then. First they went to the cabana and both sat on one chair sideways and talked for awhile. He told her how nice the thought her parents were and she wanted to know what her mother had whispered to him. He told her and she chuckled a bit.

Then Terri stood up, pulled Kevin's shirt off, pushed him back in the recliner and lay softly on top of him. He jokingly said, "Am I being seduced?" Terri smiled and said "No, I just wanted to be close to you and enjoy the hair on your chest." He responded, "Well that's a first."

They made out for awhile and he stated it was going to be lonely the next two days without her. She let him know that she was sorry to be leaving.

Around midnight she announced she had better head back to the condo. She had to pack and get a few hours of sleep. Kevin stood up, put his shirt back on and walked her to the condo. At the entrance he kissed her passionately and a small tear rolled down his cheek. Terri was surprised to see that but it assured her that he was sincere about everything he had told her.

He kissed her again. Then she walked to the door, turned around, smiled and winked at him. Kevin responded, "Call me, you have my number." He walked the beach back to his motel. There was a half moon and lots of stars. The ten minute walk took him thirty minutes as he was thinking of Terri and wondering when he would see her again.

He went in the motel room and the guys were still out partying. He set his phone alarm for 5:30 and went to bed. It took him an hour to fall asleep.

CHAPTER 11

His alarm went off at 5:30. He sat up, rubbed his eyes and went into the bathroom to wash his face and brush his teeth. He went out and got his clothes off the chair that he had neatly put there earlier. He dressed and noticed Frank wasn't there. He supposed he had hooked up with some girl and spent the night with her.

Kevin left and took off down the road to the condo. It was about ten minutes until six when he arrived. He saw Mr. Carter loading suitcases in the back of the SUV. He waited until Mr. Carter went back inside and got a little closer. In a few minutes they all came out and threw a few things in the back and started getting in. Kevin could hardly stand the thought of Terri leaving. He approached her cautiously so not to startle her. She turned and right in front of everyone threw herself into his arms and kissed him madly. They said their goodbyes. She got in and rolled down the window. He stuck his head in and kissed her one last time.

Mr. Carter had started the car and began to pull away. Terri hung out the window waving and Kevin threw her a kiss. He stood totally immobile until they were out of sight. He teared up, his heart beating fast and headed back to the motel. When he got there he went into the lobby and got a cup of coffee. He went to the room patio, sipped a little coffee and stared into space. He just kept thinking about Terri and wondering when he would see her again. He knew he had two lonely days left at the beach before heading back.

CHAPTER 12

The next morning he woke up around eight and went outside. He actually walked to the snack shack in his boxers and t-shirt without even realizing. They were getting ready to open. By eight-thirty they raised their awnings. The lady asked him what he wanted and if he had a rough night since he wasn't dressed. He looked down and realized he was wearing his navy blue boxers, but he had grabbed a ten dollar bill so he ordered an egg and bacon sandwich and a large orange juice. Since he really wasn't dressed, he took it and headed back to the motel. He sat on the patio, ate his breakfast and went inside to put on his swim trunks and flip flops. All his buddies were snoring away. He headed to the beach, dove in and swam so far out that he was barely visible. He turned around and drifted back to the shore with the waves.

When he got to the shore, he lay face down in the sand, not moving an inch. A jogger came by and nudged him with his foot and said "Hey man, are you alright?" Kevin rolled over and answered "Yes man, I'm fine." The jogger continued his run. Kevin laid there for a bit and then decided to head back to the motel and sit under the patio umbrella for some shade.

CHAPTER 13

He sat there looking into space and soon Jake and one of the other guys came out and told Kevin they were headed for McDonalds and wanted to know if he would like something. He told them that he had already eaten.

When they returned, Frank and the other friend had joined Kevin on the patio. They scarfed down the breakfast and headed to the beach. Jake stayed back to see what was going on with Kevin. It was their last day there. Jake told him he thought he was love sick with that Terri gal he had brought to the patio that morning when Jake sat there with a terrible hangover. Kevin admitted to Jake that he was in love with Terri and how they almost instantly were very fond of each other. He also told him about the fishing trip with her dad and the two dinners he had spent with her family. He also confided that he liked her parents and thought they liked him too. Jake told him to get over it, grab a beer and come to the beach with him and the rest of the guys.

Kevin did as Jake requested and joined them on the beach for a couple hours. He played some beach volleyball and went for a swim. By four that afternoon he was back in the room packed up for the trip home. He took a shower, fell across the bed and went to sleep.

Frank came in about six-thirty and noticed Kevin sleeping so he quietly took a shower and shaved. The smell of his cologne and Frank fumbling around for some clean clothes to put on woke Kevin. He told Kevin that Jake had mentioned Terri to him.

Frank begged, "Come on Kevin, get up and let's go out and have some fun tonight". Kevin responded, "Only if you agree to sleep here tonight so we can get a decent start home in the morning or we will leave you here." Frank agreed.

About that time, Jake and the other two showed up so they could clean up to go out. They were already half drunk. Frank said, "See what I mean, I may need your help tonight."

Kevin put on the jeans he had worn to dinner with Terri and her parents and a plain white t-shirt and sandals. Frank put on dark jean cut-offs with a yellow tank top and navy blue flip flops. Kevin could tell that Frank had shaved his chest and he had muscles showing everywhere, even his six-pack that was obvious under his tight tank top. The other three guys dressed in previously worn clothes and flip flops. Frank immediately got out his expensive cologne and sprayed it on the three of them.

Frank drove to a quick place to eat and then they headed to the bar they were at the night before. There were a lot of chicks there and they all started making the rounds except for Kevin. He just sat at the bar and ordered a beer. There was an older man sitting next to him observing all the college people. He asked Kevin why he wasn't mingling with the rest. Kevin told him that he was not in the mood. With that the gentleman stated, "Oh a girlfriend at home, hey?" And Kevin responded, "Not at home, but yes I have a girl.

At least I hope so." With that the older gentleman bought Kevin another beer and stated, "Well for your sake, I hope it works out."

The girls were flocking around Frank. He was so deeply tanned, he looked like a lifeguard that lived on the beach. Girls always seemed to go for the lifeguard type. Pretty soon, Kevin went for a long walk and came back to the bar around one-thirty. He found Frank and told him they had better start rounding up the other three and get back to the motel. So by two-thirty in the morning they had all three in the van and Kevin drove back to the motel.

They had to undress Jake and get him on the floor. The other two stripped down to their boxers and went to bed. Frank made sure that he and Kevin slept in the same bed because he didn't want to smell beer breath all night. Both Kevin and Frank brushed their teeth and went to bed. By then it was three in the morning.

Kevin awoke by himself at eight and got up. He tried to wake up Frank but he was snoring away. He went outside to the lobby and got a sweet roll, coffee, juice and then went back to the patio. The dolphins were again swimming by and Kevin was sad that it was the last morning he would get to see them.

About nine-fifteen, Frank walked out and asked Kevin to go get him a coffee and he would start trying to get the others up and moving.

When Kevin returned he grabbed three large trash bags from the office. He walked back to the room to find it a disaster. He handed Jake and the other two guys the trash bags and said "Come on, let's get going." Kevin and Frank loaded their bags and pretty soon here came the rest with their stuff. They all five went to the office and checked out and got in the van. Kevin said he would drive and Frank sat up front. The rest piled in the back and all fell asleep in ten minutes. Kevin headed for the highway. They drove by the condo where Terri stayed and he thought about the morning she left and remembered how she had kissed him in front of God and her parents.

Frank suggested they drive until some of them woke up and were hungry. A few hours later they awoke and were hungry. Kevin saw a Wendy's sign for the next exit. They went to the drive-thru and then kept on driving. An hour later Kevin pulled into a gas station for gas and all five used the restroom. They split the cost of the gas. Frank offered to drive but Kevin declined and got in the driver's seat. All the guys went to sleep. Kevin was glad and knew he could concentrate on Terri. He was wondering what she was doing and why she hadn't called him.

After four more hours, everyone woke up and stated they were hungry. Kevin saw a truck stop coming up and pulled off the highway. They used the restroom, got a table and looked at menus'. There was a buffet and salad bar for $9.50 so they decided to eat the buffet. Kevin and Frank picked out a healthy dinner and the rest had odds and ends. After filling up, they headed out to the van. Frank offered to drive and Kevin agreed. He was ready for a nap.

Kevin fell asleep quickly. When he woke up, to his surprise it was already ten at night. He asked Frank if he wanted him to drive and Frank told him he was doing fine. Kevin went back to sleep. About two hours out of Springfield everyone needed a bathroom break and the van needed gas too. They all bought a soft drink except for

Kevin. He had his usual iced tea with lemon. When they left the station, Jake insisted that he drive. After all, the van was his mothers. Kevin sat in the front to keep Jake intact of driving.

They pulled into the dorm about one-thirty in the morning. They were exhausted and decided to unload in the morning so they all headed up to their rooms to hit the sack. The dorm was practically empty but others would probably start arriving on Saturday and Sunday.

Kevin got a good night sleep. He woke up around ten and decided to do some laundry. The laundry mat was in the dorm basement. He threw everything in a basket and headed downstairs. He sorted through the clothes downstairs and had some of Jake's clothes too. He loaded three washers and began the wash.

He sat down and figured it was a good idea to call his parents to let them know he was safe and sound back at school. His mom answered and she was pleased they had a good time and with no problems. He didn't mention Terri because he wasn't sure if anything would become of them.

Then the washers were finished and he threw it all into two dryers. He left and went to a nearby café by campus to get a bite to eat. When he returned he stopped by the room and Jake had just woke up. He grabbed a few hangers and headed back to the laundry area. His clothes were finished drying so he folded them and hung a few shirts when Frank appeared to wash some clothes too. Kevin had Frank's two nice polo's hanging on the rack and Frank said "Those look like my shirts." Kevin said they were and gave them to Frank.

Kevin headed up to his room to put away his clean clothes. Jake was gone and Kevin assumed he had gone to get something to eat. Jake returned an hour later and was getting ready to go home which was 40 miles away. He needed to take his mom's van back, pickup his older model Ford and get his mom to do his laundry. He told Kevin that he would be back on Sunday.

On Jake's way out of town he stopped at the car wash and gave the van a quick wash and vacuum. He checked the gas gauge and felt there was enough to get home.

Kevin was rather glad to have time to be alone. He kept thinking about changing his major and then was consumed with the thought of Terri. He was surprised that she had not contacted him. He wanted to call information to get her parents' land phone number but for the time being, decided not to.

He set at his desk and decided to do some studying for the upcoming classes on Monday. He read Sociology for a couple hours and then worked on an English paper that was due at the end of the week.

He then took a nap and woke up about six that night. He called Frank to see if he wanted to go get a bite to eat. Frank said he was in so they met in front of the dorm and walked to the parking lot where Kevin's jeep was parked. They went to a hamburger place that also made great chili. After they ate Frank suggested a movie so they went to the theater to see a new release. They returned to the dorm around eleven and Kevin went straight to bed. He slept until nine the next morning and of course dreamed of Terri almost the entire night. He ate a granola bar for breakfast and got a cup of coffee out of the machine in the dorm lounge. He tried studying more but could not concentrate so he took a break. He went for a walk to a nearby park and joined some guys in a game of softball. Afterwards, he walked back to campus and drove around Springfield for a while. He found himself driving through the Drury campus and thinking how terrific it would be if Terri came to school there the next year. He drove past the dorm Mrs. Carter had made a deposit on. He parked in front of it and imagined himself walking in to pick Terri up for a date.

He then went to a sandwich shop and ordered a sandwich, chips and his usual iced tea with lemon. He decided to go to the city lake and have a picnic by himself. It was a gorgeous, warm day for the end of March in Springfield. There were several families at the park lake having a good time. He sat on the hood of his car overlooking the lake and ate his sandwich. He felt so sad but knew he had to get out of that mood. Later Kevin returned to the dorm and watched TV in the lounge and then went to his room to get some sleep.

CHAPTER 14

Kevin woke up around ten the next morning very hungry. He took a quick shower, dressed and headed to the café by campus. He decided to splurge and had an egg and cheese omelet, biscuits and gravy, coffee and juice. After feeling full from breakfast, he returned to the dorm to study. He was so involved in his studies that he didn't realize the time. About four o'clock, Jake came barreling in with his clean clothes and two sacks of food his mom had sent back with him.

Kevin was actually glad to see him because he needed a distraction from studying. Jake put his clothes away and loaded up their small refrigerator with food. He said he had a good visit with his parents. They sat and talked for a couple hours. Jake had stopped to buy a six-pack on the way back with his fake ID. He wanted Kevin to join him in a beer. Kevin rapidly agreed; he was sick of studying. After a couple of beers, Jake pulled food from the refrigerator and they ate supper in the dorm; sandwiches, potato salad and even brownies for dessert, thanks to Jake's mom.

After they ate, Jake took off to visit some other guys in the dorm. Kevin went upstairs to Frank's room to see what he was doing. He walked in unannounced and found

Frank's shirt and shoes off making out with a cute redhead. So he left and went elsewhere.

By then the dorm was buzzing with guys getting back from spring break. There was music blaring which made Kevin glad he had studied earlier when the dorm was quite. He retreated to his room and a couple guys walked by and wanted to know how his trip to Florida had gone. He told them it was great. Then he closed the door and started reading a book. By ten that night he was getting sleepy so he undressed and went to bed.

Before Kevin fell asleep, Jake returned. He got undressed and also went to bed. Jake's first class was at nine the next morning but Kevin didn't have class until ten.

Jake woke up at eight, took a shower, shaved and headed for the cafeteria. Of course Kevin woke up early too with all the noise Jake was making. After Jake left, Kevin got up, took a shower, shaved, dressed, grabbed his backpack and headed for the cafeteria. Jake had finished eating and was heading to class. Frank was having breakfast at a table nearby so Kevin joined him. After breakfast they headed to class.

Kevin's second class was a math course which his advisor taught. Kevin made an appointment to meet with him the next day and took off to the cafeteria for lunch. He found lots of friends there. They ate and talked for awhile and then he headed to his next class. After two more classes he headed to his dorm room to finish the English paper. About the time he was finished it was five-thirty and Jake showed up wanting to go to supper.

After supper they went for a short walk around campus. Jake wanted to know if he had heard from Terri. Frustrated, Kevin told him he had not heard from her.

Kevin sat on a bench along the sidewalk but Jake headed for the dorm. Kevin's cell phone rang. He looked at the number and he was sure it was a St. Louis area code. He anxiously answered it and a very sweet voice that he was all too familiar with answered with, "How are you doing?" He was so elated that he could hardly speak. He finally responded, "I am great and I miss the hell out of you!"

She wanted to know how his classes were going. He told her they were okay "But I'm dying to see you Terri." She announced "Me too and I sure miss you and the cute hair on your chest." He laughed and responded "Okay you convinced me, I'll never shave it again just for you." She said, "Oh good, you better not."

They continued small talk for twenty minutes or so and then Terri stated that she had to go because she was leaving for a meeting and her mom would not let her take her cell phone with her. He told her that he really loved and missed her and she said "Ditto". They hung up and Kevin's eyes were watering up with glee because she had called. He walked on cloud nine all the way back to the dorm.

Kevin waked into his dorm room humming and Jake said "What are you humming about?" Kevin answered, "Oh nothing". They both settled down to their desk to study for a while but Kevin couldn't keep his mind on his studies, only Terri.

CHAPTER 15

The next morning Kevin met with his advisor about changing his mechanical engineering. His advisor was very pleased and told him that he should probably also get his masters degree. Kevin said, "Whoa! That is a long ways away and I don't know if I am committed to getting a masters degree yet". His advisor told him, "You will be much more likely to get a better job with a master's degree". Kevin thanked him and told him he would seriously think about furthering his degree. He thanked the advisor for his time.

Kevin was walking to his next class and thinking he had a lot to think about. His class was freshmen English and he had always found English to be on the easy side which is why he was carrying an A in that class. That class period the professor assigned a huge paper due in three weeks. Kevin thought, "Oh brother, more studying laid on me." But he soon accepted the assignment and went about his way.

It was noon so he headed to the cafeteria for lunch. He spotted Frank at a corner table sitting by himself so he joined him. While they were having lunch four girls walked by and flirted with Frank. He is a chick magnet.

After lunch he went to his last class that day. He was glad because he wanted to head to the dorm for a nap. When he arrived to his room, Jake was playing loud music and reading a book. Kevin asked him to turn it down because he needed a nap. Jake agreed and Kevin layed down. Before Kevin was able to fall asleep, Jake was in his bed with the book on his chest, snoring. Pretty soon Kevin fell asleep to the sound of the snoring.

It was about five o'clock and they both woke up. Jake said he was hungry and wanted to go eat. Kevin told him to wait thirty minutes and he would go with him. They ate together with a few other guy friends, laughed a great deal and filled their stomachs.

When they headed back to the dorm, Kevin decided to go for a walk. He kept thinking about Terri. "Am I falling in love with her?" he thought. He couldn't answer that question; at least not just now.

He returned to the dorm and started working on the English paper. He accessed the library on the internet and gathered quite a bit of information for his paper. He didn't want to put the paper off until the last day.

CHAPTER 16

Three weeks had passed since he had talked to Terri. One night as he was studying, his cell phone rang. He looked at the number and recognized it as Terri's mom's phone number.

Anxiously he answered, "Hello there." She wanted to know what he was doing. After talking about ten minutes she said, "My prom is coming up on May 16th. It is a Thursday night." Her school and an all boy's school have their prom together at a nice hotel. After picking out the hotel, they could only book it on a Thursday night. She questionably asked, "Do you think maybe you could come to St. Louis and take me to prom? I asked my parents and they said you could stay at our house in the guest room. And they emphasized guest room". He said, "Can I check my final schedule and I will let you know. Can I text or call your mom's phone to let you know"?

Terri said she would call him and wanted to know when he would find out his finals schedule. He told her that he would know on Monday. She told him she would call him Monday night.

Monday morning he checked out his schedule for finals and to his disappointment his last final was on Friday at nine-thirty in the morning. He was so disappointed that he went directly to the professor for that final. It was a math class and it would probably be his hardest final. But he really wanted an A because that was his major.

He asked the professor if he could take the final early because something had come up and he needed to leave town the day before. The rest of his finals were scheduled okay and he also found out that if his English paper was an A, he would not have to take the final. The math professor said he would think about his request.

That evening Terri called and wanted to know if it would work out for him to take her to prom. He told her that he had a math final on Friday at nine-thirty and had asked the professor if he could take it early. He told her the professor said he would think about it.

He told Terri he would come even if he had to drive back to school that night so he could take the final. Terri said, "Oh no, I do not want to interfere with your final". She really wanted him to come but she did not want him too tired to take the final. He explained to her that he could study beforehand and not to worry about it. The next thing he asked her, "Do I need a tuxedo or can I wear pants and a sports coat"? She responded, "You wear whatever if you can make it."

They hung up and he immediately took a pair of pants, sports coat and white shirt to the cleaner. After that, he went to shop for a really cool tie. Luckily the next day his math professor told him he could take the final at seven-thirty on Monday morning. Kevin wanted to hug him but he couldn't. He thanked the professor and left his office.

He texted Terri's mom's phone and asked if Terri could please call him. That night Terri called with lots of excitement in her voice. "What did you find out about the Friday final?" He said, "I got it moved to Monday so everything will work out".

She was so excited she could hardly talk. Then she responded with, "You can stay the weekend and I can show you the sights around St. Louis." "That would be fantastic" he replied. "I'll be there that Thursday by two in the afternoon. I need directions to your house". She gave him her address and he told her he would find it because he had navigation and it would direct him to the correct house.

He asked her, "What color is your dress"? Then she told him it was red with a little white lace. He wanted to talk longer but Terri had to hang up to have dinner with her parents.

Immediately he thought about what color corsage to get and decided on white. He called a local florist to order it and decided he would take a small cooler to keep it fresh. He also decided he would shower and shave right before he left so he wouldn't have to do that when he got there.

Soon it was finals week. He had made an A on the English paper and did not have to take that final. He studied constantly to ready himself to do well on all his finals, especially his math final.

The week came and he took the math final at seven-thirty Monday morning. When he walked out, he felt good about it and then headed to the dorm to study for the three remaining finals. On Tuesday afternoon he took another final. He had two more to go; one on Wednesday afternoon and the last on Thursday morning before he left for St. Louis.

He went to the cleaner to pick up his clothes and stopped by a burger place and grabbed a bite to eat. He returned to the dorm and carefully hung up the cleaning. The tie he had bought looked great with his sports coat. It was a medium grey and the pants were black. All of a sudden he got out his black loafers and started giving them a spit shine like one would do to their army shoes. Then he checked his other clothes and decided he better head to the laundry so he would have all clean clothes to pick from for his weekend in St. Louis with Terri.

He knew he had to return to school to move out of the dorm. The deadline was that Sunday at midnight.

After he finished his laundry he decided to pack. It was May so he packed shorts, t-shirts, tennis shoes and even sandals. He also threw in a pair of jeans, khakis and a polo incase Terri's parents took them out to dinner. He had never been to St. Louis before and was excited about visiting there but his number one reason was to be with Terri.

The Wednesday final went well. He figured he probably made a B. He went back to the dorm. He was packed for the weekend and was throwing stuff into a trash bag and a couple of boxes getting ready to move home.

He would be in Pella for the summer and working mostly for his dad but also helping his mom at the craft shop. Well, the last final was over at eleven on Thursday morning. He headed to the dorm to shower and shave. He told Jake about the weekend coming up in St. Louis with Terri and Jake seemed pleased.

Jake was headed home the next day for the summer so they said their goodbyes. Kevin loaded up his jeep and was careful how he hung his clothes.

He stopped for gas to fill up the tank and got a free car wash. Then he ran through a fast food drive-thru to get a sandwich. He ordered an extra large iced tea with lemon to drink on the way. By then it was eleven or so and he knew he would not make it to Terri's by two as he had told her.

He arrived at Terri's parents at three-thirty and knew that he and Terri were going to dinner with some of her friends; including Sally and her date.

As he drove up into Terri's driveway she rushed out of the house looking so beautiful. He stepped out of the jeep and she grabbed him and kissed him so hard that he almost could not breathe.

She said, "I am so glad to see you Kevin and I can't wait for you to meet some of my friends". She helped him get his luggage out of the jeep and they went into the house. It was much bigger than his parents house and he figured it would be.

Terri showed him to the guest room. Her parents were not home but she knew they would be there soon. In twenty minutes Mr. and Mrs. Carter were there. Mr. Carter came in, shook Kevin's hand and welcomed him to their home. Mrs. Carter came over to him and gave him a gentle hug and told him she was glad to see him.

All of a sudden Kevin felt comfortable being there. Terri announced she had to go get ready and asked her mom to help her. Kevin then remembered the corsage was in his jeep. He went out, opened the cooler and it looked as good as when he put it in there. He took it into the house and asked Mr. Carter if he could put it in the refrigerator. Mr. Carter said sure and pointed the way to the kitchen. Then he came back to the living room and told Mr. Carter he had better get ready for Terri's prom. Mr. Carter told him to go ahead and that he would be taking lots of pictures before they left. Then Mr. Carter said, "Thanks Kevin for coming. I sure am glad you are here." Kevin was overwhelmed with that statement.

Kevin went upstairs to the guest room and started getting ready for the evening. Then he went downstairs and Mr. Carter started taking pictures of him. Twenty minutes later or so Terri and her mom came down. Terri looked magnificent. She had slightly curled her hair and looked like a princess who belongs in a Disney movie. Kevin could not even speak because it took his breath away.

Mr. Carter spoke up, "You look magnificent sweetheart. What do you think Kevin"? Kevin stood still and his eyes ready to pop out of his head. He finally spoke, "Oh Terri, you are the girl of my dreams. You are so beautiful." Her parents started giggling at his responses.

About that time a limo drove up and Mr. Carter said, "You better get going, here's the limo". Several pictures were taken by Mr. Carter before, during and after they got in.

Kevin said, "What's this?" Terri responded, "Oh it is all my dad's doing. He even made a reservation on The Hill at a very nice restaurant."

They settled into the limo and the driver told them to help themselves to a soft drink and hors d'oeuvres. Low and behold, Mr. Carter made sure there was iced tea with lemon.

The driver asked Terri, "890 south Flora street next right?" Terri responded with a yes. She then told Kevin that they were going to pick up Sally and her date Lon. Terri told Kevin that she and Sally had to go to their senior prom together and that he would surely like Lon and that he was a great guy.

They picked up Sally and Lon at Sally's house. Of course her parents came out to take pictures outside of the limo and after they were inside. Kevin was introduced to Sally's parents. He kind of took a liking to Lon and the girls thought their dates had hit if off since the conversation was going so easy.

They arrived at the restaurant in about twenty minutes. Kevin said, "I haven't eaten at such an elaborate place. I hope I won't embarrass you." Terri replied, "Don't worry you won't, you couldn't embarrass me if you tried."

They all split a crab appetizer and Caesar salad. The guys had a steak and the girls some sort of shrimp dish. They were too full for dessert so Kevin asked for the check. The waiter informed them that the check was already taken care of along with a generous tip. Kevin looked at Terri knowing that her dad had something to do with it. So he asked and she responded, "You know my dad."

Back in the limo they were headed to the hotel where the prom was being held. They took the elevator to the second floor and it was a magnificent ballroom decorated to the hilt. Kevin leaned over to Terri and said, "This is quite different from my proms held in the school gym back in Iowa." Terri laughed, kissed him gently and said "I really want you to have fun and enjoy yourself."

Terri's friends were all coming up to meet her date and whispering to her how hot he was. Kevin really didn't feel underdressed because about half of the guys were dressed similar to him. Even Lon wore a sports coat and slacks. Kevin was relieved at that when he and Sally joined them in the limo.

Kevin enjoyed dancing and hoped Terri did too. So he asked her to dance and the two of them looked like professional dancers out on the huge dance floor. They even looked so good together that a few people were coming around just to watch them.

They really had a great time at the prom. Kevin, Terri, Sally and Lon said their goodbyes to all the girls' friends and then took the elevator down to the front of the hotel. Kevin spotted their limo driver as he was pulling up to the curb. They had no plans for the evening so Sally asked the driver to take them by the St. Louis arch. When they drove by it Kevin looked at it in wonder. He had only seen it in pictures which didn't do it any justice.

Terri told him that in the morning she was planning on taking him there and that they would ride an elevator to the top. Kevin was absolutely flabbergasted. After a limo tour of downtown St. Louis, Terri told the driver to take them home. They first dropped off Sally and Lon. Then they headed to Terri's parents house. Kevin tried to tip the driver but the driver told him Mr. Carter had already taken good care of him.

He pulled in the drive and let them out of the limo. Both Terri and Kevin thanked him and headed up the steps to her house. Kevin asked if they could sit outside for a bit before going inside. Terri said "sure, let's sit on the swing." So they settled into the swing and he started thanking her for a great evening and telling her how much fun he had.

"How can I thank your dad for everything?" Terri replied, "Just shake his hand and thank him. My dad is a wonderful person and I imagine that he will be extremely pleased about all he provided so that we would have a great evening." "Your dad is something else," Kevin announced. Terri laughed and told him "he has liked you since our fishing trips in Florida." Then Terri snuggled into Kevin's arms and she kissed him passionately. He was kissing her back as passionately.

It was about 1:30 in the morning when Terri announced they had better go in and get some sleep. She wanted to take him up in the arch and maybe go to the zoo and planetarium which were all popular sites in St. Louis. So they kissed again and then went inside. As soon as the door closed her mom flew down the stairs to greet them. She curiously asked, "Well, how was prom? Did you have a good time?" Terri told her to come upstairs and help her get out of her gown. So Kevin headed to the guest room saying his goodnights and thanking Mrs. Carter for all she and her husband had done to make it so special. He stood in the doorway and Terri and her mom disappeared into Terri's room. Her mom kept questioning her about the evening and all Terri could talk about was what a great dancer Kevin was. She told her mom that people crowded around them to watch.

Kevin got undressed, went into his private bathroom and washed his face, brushed his teeth and then went to bed. It wasn't long and he was asleep and dreaming of Terri and their marvelous evening.

Terri had to encourage her mom to go on to bed and they could talk tomorrow. Terri fell asleep and had dreams of Kevin and the evening they had together.

Kevin awoke about eight the next morning. He jumped out of bed, took a shower and shaved. The he put on shorts, t-shirt, tennis shoes and went looking for Terri. He found

Terri and her dad in the kitchen and politely asked, "Can I join you?" Mr. Carter replied, "You are as welcome as the flowers in May." Terri and Kevin chuckled and he joined them for a cup of coffee. However, Terri was having hot tea.

Mr. Carter said, "Terri is telling me about prom last night and what a great time she had. She also remarked what a good dancer you are." Kevin blushed and responded with, "Well I have always enjoyed dancing and my mom started dancing with me when I was very young. In fact, I was voted best dancer in my high school graduating class."

Terri wanted to know if they also voted a girl as best dancer. Kevin said, "Yes, her name was Debbie and we looked pretty good on the dance floor". He was shy to have admitted this. Terri wanted to know if he dated Debbie. But Kevin explained she was going steady with another classmate but he hated dancing. So she danced with me.

Mr. Carter interrupted with, "how was the restaurant last night and did you enjoy the food?" Kevin stood on his feet and shook Mr. Carter's hand and said, "Both were wonderful and I can't thank you enough for all you did." Mr. Carter sat in his chair grinning and told Kevin that it was his pleasure.

Terri announced that she and Kevin needed to get going because of all the sights she was going to show him. Mrs. Carter strolled in the kitchen and offered to fix breakfast. Terri told her they would get a bite on the way to the arch and gave both her parents a kiss and hug before they left.

Mr. Carter poured herself a cup of coffee, sat down and said, "I think she really likes that guy and it is a good thing that we do too."

CHAPTER 17

Terri insisted on driving her car, a Volkswagon convertible, because she knew her way around St. Louis and wouldn't have to be giving him directions. He put the top down and they were off. They arrived at the arch just as it was opening. She found a parking place on the riverfront close by. They walked into the ground level and Kevin was so amazed of the whole atmosphere. She hurriedly got in line to get tickets and was told it would be fifteen minutes before entering the cargo elevators that took them to the top. Then they stood in line to wait. Kevin wanted to pay for the tickets but Terri wouldn't let him.

It wasn't long and they were on board to go to the top. When they got up there Kevin said, "Does this thing seem to be swaying a little or is it just me?" Terri answered, "Sometimes on windy days you can feel the sway."

They looked on the east side first and could see what he thought was most of Illinois. It was an absolutely beautiful clear sunny day. Then they move to the west side. Terri pointed out to him some of the downtown attractions. Then all of a sudden he blurted, "Oh my gosh, there is Busch stadium and you can see right into it". Terri said, "Wait until you see it up close and personal". Kevin asked if they were going there next. She said, "Not until tomorrow night. The Cardinals are in town and dad got tickets for all of us". "What?" Kevin yelled. "I have never been to a professional baseball game in my life and the Cardinals were always my favorite. That is terrific."

After about thirty minutes or so they rode down to the bottom floor. Terri took him through the museum and they watched the video of the arch being built. When they left, Terri said, "I am hungry, let's go to McDonalds". There was a riverfront McDonalds down from where she had parked so they walked. Kevin said, "If that doesn't beat all, a floating McDonalds on the Mississippi river". They went inside, got their food and went out on the deck to eat.

Kevin exclaimed, "Where next?" Terri said, "I think we'll head for the zoo. It is free admission and lots to see".

Twenty minutes later they arrived at the zoo and Terri suggested they ride the train for a small fee and he could see practically everything there. When they got off the train they walked down to where the seals were in the outdoor pool. It was feeding time and Kevin got a kick out of how they came jumping to receive a fresh fish meal.

Then they walked around and saw lots of other animals. Kevin really liked the lions, giraffes and bears. Then they got something to drink and headed back to the parking lot. When they arrived at her car and she started to get in he said "Wait a minute, I just realized that I haven't kissed you all day." So he held her dearly and passionately kissed her. She responded, "Can I have more of that?" He immediately kissed her and hugged her several more times.

They finally got into the car and Terri headed to the Planetarium. They arrived just in time to get a ticket to the stars and sky and even different shapes of the moon and what they were called. Kevin had never been to such a place and he was amazed.

When they got back to the car Terri told him that they had better head home because her dad was barbequing and would want to eat dinner at seven sharp.

They got there at six, greeted her parents and went upstairs to freshen up. Kevin washed his face, brushed his teeth, combed his hair, put on a clean t-shirt and a spritz of cologne. He headed toward the stairs but Terri's door was open. He pushed in and said, "Are you in here?" He heard her giggle and then she told him to come on in. She walked out of her bathroom wearing a short skirt, a lovely blouse and those cute strappy sandals her mom had bought her in Florida. She about took Kevin's breath away and without saying a word, he approached her and gave her a long deep kiss. She announced, "Wow, how hot was that? We better head downstairs before my parents come looking for us."

They went downstairs and into the kitchen. Her dad had the steaks marinating and the grill going outside. Mrs. Carter was busy making a salad and twice baked potatoes, at her husband's request. Mr. Carter took the steaks and Kevin outside with him and asked Terri to help her mother. He asked Kevin how he liked his steaks and he told him medium. Mr. Carter put only one steak on and told him that was Terri's because for some reason she liked hers more done. He handed Kevin a pair of tongs and told him in five minutes he should put two more steaks on the grill and in another five minutes he should put the last steak on because he liked his rare. He then said he was going inside to finish off the shrimp kabobs to grill.

Kevin was surprised that he trusted him with such fine steaks. However, he was very much at ease with the grill because when he was at home he did most of the grilling.

When it was about time to put the last steak on Mr. Carter returned with the kabobs and two beers. He asked Kevin to join him with a beer. Kevin was reluctant at first but decided to accept. After all, the first time he had met the man he had drank a Bloody Mary with him and for breakfast no less.

Kevin put the remaining steak on and checked the other three to see if they were ready to turn. Mr. Carter came over and took over the grill and put the kabobs on. He told Kevin to sit down and enjoy his beer because he didn't want to take advantage of their house guest. So Kevin without hesitating took his suggestion.

Soon Terri came out to set the table and told he dad that her mom wanted to eat outside. Mr. Carter didn't argue because it was a beautiful evening and the patio was in the shade.

Kevin thought the meal was exceptional and graciously thanked them. "Mr. Carter, you sure know how to marinate and cook great steak. And Mrs. Carter, you make the best twice baked potatoes I have ever had." Mr. Carter responded with, "Kevin, please call me James. We don't have to be so formal and call my wife Judy." Kevin felt rather odd doing that but decided he would give it a try. He had also been brought up to call your elders Mr. or Mrs. and not by the first name. When he asked Terri about it later, she said that all her friends called them by their first names. That is what they preferred.

After dinner, Mrs. Carter had another glass of wine and Mr. Carter had switched to scotch. Terri served Kevin an ice tea with lemon and instead of her usual coke, she had one too.

After about twenty minutes Terri got up to clean the table and Kevin jumped up to help. Mrs. Carter told them that she would be in in a minute to help with the dishes. Kevin asked her to sit and enjoy her wine and the wonderful evening. He would help Terri with the dishes.

After they went inside, Mrs. Carter leaned over and told her husband, "That boy is growing on me. Why do you know he even makes his bed every morning and his bathroom is spotless, like he never used it." Mr. Carter replied, "I saw the goodness in him the morning I met him on the fishing trip and liked him from the get go."

After a while they went inside and Kevin and Terri had finished the dishes and were in the family room watching television. Her parents joined them. Mr. Carter started yawning and announced he was headed for bed. Mrs. Carter told him to go ahead and she would join him in a few minutes. After she headed for the bedroom Terri suggested that she and Kevin go for a walk. It was a very beautiful neighborhood. The houses were a bit older but nice and most of them were two stories. Terri started telling Kevin who lived where and pointed out a house where she sometimes babysat.

There was an older couple rocking in their chairs on the front porch. Terri stopped to say hello and introduced Kevin to them. After they strolled away, she told Kevin that the lady used to babysit her when she was young and that she always kind of thought of her as her second grandma.

They strolled around the neighborhood for an hour or so and returned to the house. By then it was ten thirty. Terri said, "We better hit the sack, we have a busy day tomorrow with Grant's Farm and the ball game.

He gave her a big kiss on the porch before they went in. She also embraced him and the next thing you knew, they were kissing. He told her how much he adored her and thanked her for a great weekend. Then they went up to bed to their separate rooms.

He awoke around eight. He showered, shaved and finished the rest of his morning routine. He went out in the hallway and Terri had already gone downstairs. He walked into the kitchen and was greeted with a cup of coffee by Mrs. Carter. Mr. Carter was making pancakes and Terri was cooking some scrambled eggs. He could not believe he was the last to come downstairs. He apologized in hopes he had not delayed breakfast. "Not at all" replied Mrs. Carter. "I just came in the kitchen myself". She was still wearing her robe and slippers.

Mr. Carter was dressed and wanted to get to the country club. He was playing nine holes of golf with his buddies. They all got too worn out playing the full eighteen so they just played nine.

After breakfast, Kevin jumped up and started clearing the table. Terri helped him and then Mrs. Carter instructed them to go ahead and she would do the dishes. Mr. Carter was already out the door to play golf and barely said goodbye.

Terri grabbed her purse and said to Kevin, "Let's go." Mrs. Carter announced that they were leaving by four-thirty for the seven fifteen game and please arrive home in time. Terri reassured her that they would.

Kevin wanted to take his jeep but Terri insisted that she take her car. They jumped in, Terri put the top down and they were headed for Grant's Farm. When arriving, they got their tickets and boarded the train that showed them around the farm. Kevin noticed quite a few kids were there and asked Terri if this place was mostly for kids. She told him that it was for young and old alike. She then confessed that when she was a child that her parents bought her there a lot and that it was one of her favorite places in St. Louis. She couldn't wait to show him.

They ended up at this magnificent barn and there were two Clydesdale horses with their harnesses on and the Dalmatian dog. Everyone was having their picture taken with them. Terri begged Kevin to do it so they got it line.

Then after the picture they went inside. Kevin couldn't believe they were giving away free beer. But you needed an I.D. He still had his fake one but really didn't want a beer anyway. They got two cokes because they didn't have iced tea.

They saw a couple of baby Clydesdales getting their daily bath, a baby elephant that they could pet and several other animals up close. After a few hours there they loaded onto the small train and were taken to the parking lot where Terri's car was parked. After getting in the car, Terri asked him, "Did you have as good a time as I did?" Kevin winked at her and said, "Yes, of course I did, maybe even better". Before she started the car Kevin leaned over and kissed her and thanked her for a wonderful time.

She said, "We have just enough time to run by the frozen custard place before we head home. It is known throughout the state and half of Illinois." She drove off in a flurry to get there.

Upon arrival Kevin noted that it was a small building and the parking lot was almost full. There were probably forty to fifty people in line at the window. He thought to himself that this was going to take forever. Terri jumped out of the car and said, "Come on, we have to get in line." So Kevin followed and surprisingly they were only in line ten minutes until they reached the window. They gave their order, paid for it and within seconds they had their custard. Terri talked Kevin into getting a concrete and she had a sundae. They went back to her car and enjoyed the custard and then headed back to her parents' house.

Upon arrival Terri stated that her dad was home and was probably anxious to get going. They jumped out of the car, put the top up and headed into the house. Mr. Carter announced that they had fifteen minutes until they were leaving. They both rushed upstairs. Kevin went into his bathroom, splashed water on his face, added a little deodorant and cologne and brushed his hair. About that time Terri walked in and said, "I bought a gift and I want you to wear it tonight." He took it out of the bag and it was a Cardinal's t-shirt. She told him to put it on and she would meet him downstairs. So he did as he was instructed.

Mr. Carter had on khaki shorts and a white polo with a small St. Louis Cardinal's emblem. Mrs. Carter was dressed similar only in white shorts and snow white tennis shoes with red socks and Cardinal's emblem on them.

In about five minutes Terri came down wearing a t-shirt exactly like the one she had given Kevin. She was wearing white shorts and those cute strappy sandals.

They all loaded into Mr. Carter's black SUV and they were off towards downtown to see the Cardinal's game. It was a first for Kevin and he was so excited that he could hardly wait to get there.

CHAPTER 18

They arrived downtown around 4:45. Mr. Carter stated they had time to get a quick bite to eat. Terri responded, "Ok dad, let's make this a true ball park night and have hot dogs, bratwurst and nachos for dinner." Mr. Carter agreed and pulled into a parking lot and got a space. It was three blocks west to the stadium. Kevin saw the arch and was still in awe of him and Terri's trip there the day before.

They entered the stadium park and Mr. Carter led the way. He stopped by a food concession and told everyone to order up. So everyone ordered what they wanted, took their cardboard trays of food and headed for their seats. By then it was six and the game would start in just over an hour. They went down a few steps and out into the open air of the park. Mr. Carter led them to their seats which were five rows behind the Cardinal's dugout. He couldn't believe how close they were and he was so excited that he could hardly eat his bratwurst and nachos.

The players were on the field warming up and Mr. Carter said, "Give Terri your food tray and come with me." They walked down five rows and Mr. Carter hollered at one of the players standing there. He had taught him at Washington University last year. The player came over, reached up and shook Mr. Carter's hand. Mr. Carter told him he wanted an autograph for his young friend with him. The player went into the dugout and came back with a print of the entire team, signed it to Kevin, shook his hand and welcomed him to the game. Kevin was about to faint because having been a Cardinal fan for years, he knew all the players and especially was fond of the one who signed the picture. Mr. Carter thanked him and they returned to their seats to finish eating. However, Kevin was so overwhelmed he could not eat a bite. Terri was amused at Kevin's reaction. He had met the player who signed the picture and he was rather fond of the dad.

The first pitch went out and Kevin was on his feet cheering. One could tell he was a novice at a professional baseball game. He could hardly stay in his seat during the game. When the Cardinals had the bases loaded and the next batter hit a homerun for a grand slam, everyone in the stadium was cheering. The organist played and Kevin was standing in his seat yelling his head off. Terri was getting a kick out of Kevin's reactions to the game and was excited that he was enjoying himself so much.

The Cardinals won the game and the four of them were in the crowd of people leaving. Kevin hung on to his autographed picture like it was gold and protected it from the crowd more than he did Terri. Terri was quite alright with that and hung on to Kevin's arm until they got to the street.

They walked the three blocks to the parking garage and Kevin looked at the arch with all the magnificent lighting effects and he was amazed. They got to the garage, went to their black SUV and headed out into the traffic to get home.

Mr. Carter asked if anyone was hungry and wanted to stop somewhere and eat. Everyone said no they were not hungry. When they arrived Mr. Carter pulled into the garage and went straight to the kitchen to make a sandwich. He offered everyone a sandwich and the ladies declined. Mr. Carter said, "Please Kevin, won't you join me?" Kevin told him okay and with that Mr. Carter was pulling things out of the refrigerator. He made them both pastrami, cheese, tomato and lettuce sandwiches with horseradish and mayonnaise. They both sat at the counter and began to eat. Kevin got himself a glass of milk out of the refrigerator and Mr. Carter asked Kevin to get him one too.

Terri and her mom went upstairs to put on their pajamas. Kevin was having a good time with Mr. Carter when Terri returned. She said, "Mom went on to bed and told me to tell you to come on to bed." He obeyed the order and Kevin and Terri cleaned up the kitchen. Kevin told Terri that her dad made a mean pastrami sandwich.

She asked him to join her on the patio and so he did. He sat in a large chair and Terri sat in his lap. She pulled up his t-shirt and put her hand on his chest. As before, she told him she loved the hair on his chest and not to shave it. Kevin told her that he had no intention of doing that.

Soon they started hugging and kissing like maniacs. Kevin held back because he didn't want it to lead to having sex. She was a virgin and too young and he had learned his lessons two times before in the last year or so. So he slowed things down and told Terri that it was way too early in their relationship to be having sex. Terri sat up, looked him in the eyes and stated, "I respect you for that but I was hoping this would be the night." He came out with, "Terri, the time might be right but we really need to wait. But I promise it will happen someday."

Terri told him that she absolutely understood and that she respected him for being the man he was and resisting when she thought she was ready. "The time will be right and we will both know it." So he announced, "Please Terri, be patient. I don't want you to regret what we did." She responded, "Okay, I guess you are right. You always think things through until the end, more than I do and I trust your judgment."

With that, Kevin announced that they should go in and hit the sack because he had to leave in the morning to get back to school and load up to head home to Iowa. She asked him, "Do you want to attend church with us tomorrow? Sally is singing in the choir and as I hear it Lon has a terrific solo. He is a fantastic singer!"

Kevin sat there thinking about it and told her he would decide in the morning. They quietly went inside, went upstairs, he kissed her goodnight at her bedroom door and told her he would see her in the morning.

He had a difficult time falling asleep and knowing good and well he would not have time to go to church, get to Springfield, pack up his things and check out of the dorm unless he left by nine or ten at the latest.

CHAPTER 19

Kevin awoke by seven and took a shower. He made the bed and wiped down the sink and shower. He packed his bag, put hanging clothes in their hanging bag and headed downstairs with them to load his jeep. Terri heard him stirring around. She got up, put on her robe and went downstairs. Kevin had just walked back inside. She asked if he was staying for church. He told her that he was afraid he wouldn't have time.

Then they went to the kitchen and she made him coffee and for herself hot tea. As they were drinking their beverages, she asked him, "I graduate on June tenth. Can you come back for it?" He checked his calendar on his cell phone and when he saw that date he couldn't even swallow, let alone speak.

Terri said, "What is wrong?" Kevin sadly told her, "Cat's big dance recital is that night and she has a solo in a jazz routine and I promised her that I would be there." Terri sat and disappointedly said, "That's okay, if you have already promised Cat, you need to be there."

He thought it over and mentioned to Terri maybe he could work it out. He may skip the recital and come to her graduation. Terri exploded with, "Don't you disappoint your little sister. Graduation is boring anyway and the party afterwards will be with my relatives."

She convinced Kevin it was perfectly alright with her and not to worry about it.

With that, he asked her to walk him to his jeep. He gave her a big hug and thanked her for being so understanding about how much it meant to his little sister that he attend her recital.

They just stood by the jeep for a bit. He gave her a hug and told her to please thank her parents for all they did for the best weekend of his life. He bent down, gave her a very passionate kiss. Then he got in the jeep and drove off down the street. Terri watched until he was out of sight.

When he arrived in Springfield he parked at the dorm. He headed out to see if his grades were posted. He already knew he had an A in English so he headed to the Math department. He also received an A in Math, too. He headed to Sociology and in disappointment he received a B plus. His other two classes were A's too.

He went to the dorm and packed all his belongings and headed down to the jeep. He had about one more load and he was out of there. He went back in and went to Frank's room and he was long gone. "Oh well" he thought, maybe I will call him and Jake on my drive to Iowa. He loaded the last of his things and went to the office to check out. Then he headed to the gas station to fill up and he was on his way home. It was three by then so he called his mom to tell her he was finally leaving and he would be home late and not to wait up. His mom asked him to be careful driving and to wear his seat belt. He drove to Columbia and stopped for a sandwich at Subway, went to the bathroom and back in the car. He headed north on highway sixty-three and when he got to Kirksville he stopped to get more gas. He thought to himself that he should be home in six or seven hours. So it was looking like midnight before he would arrive home.

Kevin was off a little on his timing. He got to his parents a little after eleven. He grabbed his shaving kit and duffle bag and quietly went in to his room. His mom heard him because she hadn't fallen asleep yet. She went to his room, gave him a big hug and kiss and said, "I am glad you are safe and that you are home."

He told her to tell Cat to wake him before she left for school and maybe he would take her. If dad has left by then, I will go out to the site where he is building and see him.

They hugged goodnight, he stripped down to his boxers, collapsed in his bed and immediately fell asleep. He was exhausted.

CHAPTER 20

At seven fifteen the next morning Cat ran to his room, threw open the door and woke him up. However he pretended to still be asleep. She jumped on the bed and on top of him and started bouncing up and down. She said, "Come on sleepy head, wake up."

He opened one eye and looked up at her. She told him to get out bed because she wanted him to drive her to school. He threw his arms around her, gave her a big hug and told her to go on down and eat breakfast and that he would be down in a minute. "Oh by the way, has dad left for work yet?" She said no because he was waiting to see him. Cat went on her way to eat breakfast.

Kevin hurriedly dressed and went downstairs to the kitchen. His dad greeted him with open arms and gave him a huge hug and welcomed him home. His mom was making bacon and pancakes. He loved his mom's pancakes.

The four of them had breakfast and then Cat was told to go brush her teeth. She returned in ten minutes, her backpack over her shoulder and announced, "Come on big bro, take me to school." Kevin jumped up and said, "Yes ma'am." Then they were headed out the door, jumped in his jeep and off to school they went. He pulled up in front of the school, Cat leaned over and gave him a hug and kiss on his cheek and said, "I'm so glad you are home, I have missed you so much and I love you." Before he could respond, out the door she went and was running to the school building. He just sat there and watched her and grinned from ear to ear.

He returned home. His dad had left for work but his mom was still there washing up the breakfast dishes. He told her thanks for the pancakes and that no one could make pancakes like she does.

They visited about twenty minutes and he told her he had all A's and one B plus this semester. She was pleased and told him so.

Then she went to get dressed and to get ready to open her shop. Kevin went out to his jeep to unload all his stuff. He took the boxes of books to the basement and everything else to his room. He gathered up his dirty clothes and headed to the laundry room to wash his clothes. Then he went and took a shower, shaved, dressed and decided to go see his mom at her shop.

When he walked in there were two ladies there that he knew and they welcomed him home. In Pella, it seemed like you knew everyone and that gave him a warm sense of security.

He hadn't mentioned Terri or even about going to St. Louis to her prom; although he was dying to tell his dad about going to the Cardinals game at Busch Stadium. He was still trying to figure out how to tell them. He wanted it to go over okay with his parents. He was thinking maybe that evening after dinner.

He stayed at his mom's shop for quite awhile and then drove out to his dad's job site. His dad was building a huge pole barn for round bales of hay. He was amazed how large it was. His dad greeted him with, "Ready to come to work tomorrow?" Kevin responded, "Sure why not."

He headed back to town to finish his laundry and unpacking. He fixed a ham sandwich, poured a glass of milk and ate a late lunch.

Cat got off school at three so he decided to pick her up. He was early so he went to her classroom. She was so excited and announced to her teacher and the whole class, "This is my brother, Kevin." Most of them already knew that. Her teacher let her leave a little early and she and Kevin walked to the parking lot and she was holding his hand like she was a first grader instead of a fourth grader. However, Kevin loved it and was quite amused. They were rather close considering they were eight years apart in age.

He took her to the Dairy Stop and got both of them an ice cream cone. Then they stopped by their mom's shop for a bit. He asked his mom if he could start dinner for her. She told him they are going to grill hamburgers but he could make the lettuce salad. "I bought some potato salad at the deli yesterday so we'll have that too. However, you could mix up the baked beans. Do you remember how?" Kevin answered, "Are you kidding? Remember, they are my specialty?" His mom laughed and told the kids she would be home a little after five but wasn't sure what time their dad would be home but he would call and let her know. About that time her cell phone rang and it was her husband and he would be home by six. She told Kevin that he must be getting home early because he was home.

Kevin and Cat headed home. Kevin mixed up the baked beans and began to cut up the salad. Cat sat at the kitchen table and did her homework.

She told him that she was so happy he was there and would see her dance recital. She exploded, "Wait until you see me, I have a solo dance and I will be doing a jazz routine."

He asked if he could see a preview and she told him no because she wanted it to be a surprise.

So Kevin finished up the salad, put it in the refrigerator and the beans in the oven. Then he proceeded to get the hamburgers ready for the grill.

About that time his mom came home and Kevin told her that dinner was ready to go. All he had to do was grill the burgers. She told him he was a real dear for doing that.

Cat finished her homework and Kevin asked her to set the table. He really badly wanted to tell his folks about Terri and his wonderful weekend in St. Louis; especially about the Cardinals game.

His dad called and said he would be home in thirty minutes so Kevin fired up the grill. In fifteen minutes or so, he put on the burgers. His mom mixed up her salad dressing that Kevin loved.

His dad got there and dinner was ready to be served. They sat down to dinner and asked Kevin about changing his major. Kevin told them that his advisor had recommended that because he would have a better chance in the business world at getting a really good job.

Then Kevin wondered, "Should I tell them about Terri or what?"

CHAPTER 21

Terri was busy with her finals and she and her mom were planning a graduation party. Her grandmother, two aunts, the husbands and her three cousins who were all much younger than her were planning on attending her party. She was looking forward to graduating and was really wishing that Kevin would be there. However, she realized he couldn't disappoint his little sister nor did she want him to.

That night she went to her room to study but all she could think about was Kevin and how much she missed him. She thought about calling him on her mom's phone but decided against it.

She turned on her computer to check her emails. She had about twenty and as she scrolled down she noticed that one of them was from Kevin. She hurriedly clicked on it and started reading.

He wrote, "I can't tell you how much I have missed you and I think of you all the time. I also want to thank you for such a wonderful weekend and inviting me to your prom. Thank you for all the places you took me and to get to see the Cardinals game was fabulous. Your parents are so generous and welcomed me into their home like I was an old friend. I mailed them a thank you note yesterday so they should get it tomorrow. Oh Terri I miss you so and can hardly wait until we see each other again."

She quickly replied, "I miss you too. Mom is about to drive me crazy with my graduation party plans. I thought it would be small with family only but now I think she has invited a lot more people. But on the good side my Aunt Barbara will be here and I am going to ask her to keep talking to dad about me going to Drury. And maybe between her, my mom and me we will be able to convince him. It was absolutely wonderful hearing from you. Let's keep in touch and keep these emails coming. I told my dad that all I wanted for graduation was a cell phone. I think about you every day."

Kevin was still on his computer and the message came that he had new mail. He opened it and was so delighted that he got tears in his eyes and had to wait a few seconds so he could read it.

He answered back, "Let's both pray for Drury. In my heart I think it will happen. Enjoy your party even if your mom invited half of St. Louis. Miss you even more now."

CHAPTER 22

After having dinner he got up the nerve and told his parents that he had something he wanted to talk to them about. His dad said, "We are listening, go ahead."

Kevin continued telling them how he met this girl on the beach at spring break. He told them about the fishing trip with Terri and her dad and that he went to their condo that night for a fish dinner. He continued telling them all about the rest of the time he spent with Terri and her parents. He included that they were wonderful people. He then told them that she invited him to come to St. Louis for the weekend to go to her prom. His parents listened intently. She invited him to St. Louis, with her parents' permission, to attend her prom. He also added, "She and I were a hit at her prom, everyone gathered around to watch us dance." He continued, "Thanks to you and grandma I ended up being a pretty good dancer." There was no verbal response from his mom, just a smile. He continued on telling them all the places she had taken him and he told them that the highlight was going to Busch Stadium to see the Cardinals beat the Cubs.

He suddenly stopped not knowing what to say next. His dad said, "Go on." Then he told them about the limo, dinner on the hill and all the rest. He included how he had to leave early Sunday morning to get back to Springfield to his dorm room and finish loading up his belongings.

His mother said, "And then?" He answered, "What do you mean?" He continued to tell his parents how fond he was of Terri and that he really wanted her to visit Pella that summer.

His dad jumped in and said, "Well, get her up here if you are that crazy about her." Kevin was totally elated about what his dad had said. He turned to his mom and she saw the question on his face. "Sure invite her up, maybe the fourth of July weekend?"

Kevin could hardly believe his ears because he was so cautious to tell them about Terri. Then he stood up and gave both his parents a hug and thanked them for being the wonderful parents they were.

The whole time he wanted to get to the computer to email Terri. His sister had finished cleaning the table then looked Kevin straight in the eyes and pronounced, "You are not marrying her until I say so. I have to love and approve of her."

Kevin told her not to worry because marriage was a long, long way off. Cat responded, "That is good. I love you dear brother Kevin." Then he responded, "And I love you more than you love me."

They were about to depart to the patio but Kevin excused himself because he was dying to email Terri.

He told her on email that he wanted to invite her to Iowa and that his parents suggested she come over July fourth weekend. He then wrote that she could take a plane to Des Moines and he would pick her up.

He sat there and stared at his computer for awhile. Nothing came back in thirty minutes so he joined his family on the patio. He told his parents that he emailed Terri and invited her but didn't get a response yet. Cat said, "Why don't you just call her cell phone and ask?" He answered that she didn't have a cell phone and the internet was his only contact. Cat said, "Why doesn't she have a cell phone?" Kevin responded, "Because her parents won't get her one." But he was sure hoping they would get her one for graduation. And with that, Cat told her parents that she really needed a cell phone. Her parents told her she had to wait until she was fourteen.

The family went indoors and had chocolate sundaes for dessert and Kevin hurried off to his room as soon as his sundae was devoured. He checked his email and there was a message from Terri. She told him that she would talk it over with her parents. He so badly wanted to respond and tell her he loved her but decided he should wait for that.

A week went by and he and his parents went to Cat's dance recital. He was so very much impressed with Cat's solo dance. He was amazed and after the recital presented his little sis with a bouquet of flowers; all the time waiting to hear from Terri about the fourth.

He and his family went in the house and all headed for bed. About that time his cell phone rang and he recognized the area code to be a St. Louis number. He answered and said, "Hello is this Terri?" And she answered, "How did you know?"

Terri had finally gotten a cell phone for graduation and could not wait to call Kevin. Kevin knew that Mr. Carter would come through with Terri's request. They talked a bit and he asked her if she had talked to her parents about coming to Iowa. She told him not yet but promised to do so soon. It had been a busy time and her aunt had put the pressure on about Drury. So their conversation almost ended with that but Kevin told her he would call or text her everyday and enough with the emails.

CHAPTER 23

The next day he sent her a simple text stating, "I sure miss you more and more everyday and I sure am hoping you can come for the fourth weekend."

In an instant she responded back, "Miss you too and I plan on talking to my parents about coming to Iowa at dinner tonight. Keep your fingers crossed."

He answered, "They are plus my toes, arms and legs."

Then he went to his mom's shop to see if she needed anything. She was glad to see him. She wanted his help to move some of the displays around. There were two ladies in shopping so they waited until they left. They both walked out carrying a bag full. Their sale totaled $89.00. Then he and his mom moved a few displays around and she asked him to go in the back, get the mop and clean the floor where the shelves had been moved.

She had a great deal of things in red, white, and blue representing the fourth of July for sale. Kevin told his mom that he was very impressed with the way the store was set up and the upcoming holiday merchandise.

Then she put an out to lunch sign on the door and they headed to a café down the street. Kevin loved this little café that he had gone to his whole life. He knew the owner and all the waitresses. When he walked in, they all came up and he even got a couple hugs. He and his mother ordered a spinach salad and iced tea with lemon, of course. Several people came and went and many of them stopped by his table to say hello and welcome him home for the summer.

After lunch his mom went back to the shop he and went to visit his best friend from high school. Craig, his friend, did not go to college. His parents needed him to stay home to help run the family business, a furniture store. Craig's dad was suffering with a severe breathing problem and doctors told him to only work at the store two or three hours a day. His mom was left there to do all the bookwork with only one part-time employee. So Craig stayed to help his mom and less than one year from getting out of high school was running the entire operation at the store.

Craig was African American and lots of people thought that his family could not afford to send him to college or that his grades weren't good enough to get into a college. It was all gossip just because of his race. This was a terrible misconception which always angered him when he thought about it. He and Craig had been best friends since eighth grade and Craig was one of the star players on the football team in high school.

After a visit with Craig, Kevin headed out to his dad's job site. His dad was taking a short break to get a cold drink as well as the crew. It gave Kevin a chance to visit with his dad.

His dad asked him if he was ready to go to work in the morning. Kevin told him that he was ready. He enjoyed the small salary that his dad paid him. When he worked for his mom it was also free because she needed him to help.

After his visit with his dad, he told him that he would be ready to go to work and that if everything worked out with Terri coming he may want a couple of extra days off over the fourth to show her around.

Kevin went home and read a few chapters in a book he started. Then he got on the computer to register for classes in the fall. His advisors told him he had to take a couple of classes in Economics for his new major that he had yet to declare. After figuring out what he needed to take, he clicked on finished. He knew it would take a few days to find out if his schedule would work or not.

Then he went to the kitchen, checked out the refrigerator, and saw some pork ribs. He called his mom and asked her if he should start the ribs. She said sure and go ahead and fix them however you want. He took the ribs out and boiled them in some beer but saved a bit to sip on.

He got out the potatoes, an onion and some garlic powder. He was planning on making a dish that he learned in boy scouts. He always called them "Boy Scout potatoes".

He then went to his room to dig out his work boots and check to see if his work jeans and t-shirts advertising his dad business on the back were there. They were navy blue with white lettering on the back stating Ruhele Construction and the phone number. There were four of them all clean and hanging in his closet. He was set with what to wear to work the next day.

He then decided to peel the potatoes and peel and chop up an onion. He folded them tightly in foil with butter and the powdered garlic and added a little bit of Parmesan cheese. He had the grill heating and took the potato mixture and put it on the grill. Then he went inside and found everything he needed to make a green bean casserole that they usually had on holidays. He decided to make it for dinner and mixed it up and put it in the oven. About twenty minutes had passed and he went out to put them on the grill. He went back inside and got the barbeque sauce, mixed in a few extras like a little beer, put it in a long baking dish and headed for the grill. He put the pan on the top rack and turned the ribs. They were browning nicely so he brushed a little sauce on them. He went back inside. Cat had walked in and was looking for him. He told her to get her homework done and then she could join him in the kitchen to set the table and help him finish dinner.

He went out to the grill in about twenty minutes and took foil with him. He put the ribs in the sauce and covered it with the grill and left it on the top shelf. He turned the grill to low, turned the potato mixture over and went back inside. He checked the green bean casserole and it was bubbling so he added a can of onion rings. He checked his mom's pantry and found some rolls from the bakery. He wrapped them in foil and put them into the oven.

Cat entered and announced that her homework was done and that she only had four days of school left and two more days after that until her dance recital. She ran over and gave Kevin a hug and said, "What's for dinner? And where is mom?" He told her that their mom would be a little late. He then asked Cat to set the table and make some iced tea and to cut up a lemon.

She answered, "Okie dokie pokie." And then she laughed. Kevin was very amused with her.

Then he checked his cell phone for missed calls or text. There were none. So he said a silent prayer that Terri's parents would let her come for the fourth.

About that time his mom got home and asked, "How is dinner doing?" He replied, "Almost ready. I made a green bean casserole like you make on holidays. I thought it sounded good." She responded, "Wonderful, how are the ribs doing?"

He headed out to the grill to stir the ribs around in the sauce, covered them again, flipped the foil of potatoes, gave them a squeeze and decided they were close to done so he moved them to the top shelf next to the ribs.

He had finished off the left over beer before his mom came home. His mom said she would call his dad to see when he was coming home. He answered and told her that he was in the driveway. He came in and greeted everyone, grabbed a beer and headed for the shower.

He returned twenty minutes later with shorts and a t-shirt on and an empty beer can. He wanted to know what was for dinner.

His wife told him to wait and that Kevin had prepared the entire meal. Cat jumped up and stated, "I made the iced tea and set the table." Then Kevin told her that she had been a great help.

He went out to retrieve the ribs and potatoes. He sat them on top of the stove, got the green beans and rolls out of the oven and started dishing things up. He put a couple of hot pads on the table; one for the hot rib pan and one for the casserole. He then put the rolls in a basket, put the potato mixture in a bowl and set both on the table and said, "Dinner is served."

His parents raved about how fabulous dinner was. Dad said, "Maybe I should have sent you to a culinary school instead of a college." Kevin responded, "No dad, I don't think so. I enjoy doing grilling and a few other aspects of cooking but that's all." His dad told him "I'm just kidding."

Dinner was over and dishes were cleaned by his mom and Cat. His cell phone rang and he ran to answer it.

CHAPTER 24

"Hi Terri" he said immediately. She answered him and told him that she had good news. Her parents said she could come to Iowa for the fourth. Her dad was going to make reservations on Thursday and a return flight on Tuesday.

Kevin was so excited that he could hardly talk. He finally told her that he could hardly wait to tell his parents and Cat because they were all anxious to meet her. She told him that after her dad made the plane reservations and she knows the times, she would let him know.

"Oh Terri" he stated, "I can hardly wait for you to get here." He also concluded, "Fourth of July is a big deal in Pella as it is in St. Louis but people around here love it."

Terri told him that she had figured that and was still anxious to come.

The day came and he was about to leave for Des Moines to the airport. It was a very dark, cloudy day and storms were predicted. As he drove to Des Moines, the sky started thundering and lightning. He started to worry about Terri and her flight. He arrived at the airport and a pouring rain came down with huge gust of wind. He got into the airport, checked the boards and it said Terri's flight was on time. Time passed slowly and it was posted time for her flight to land. He checked out the boards and it relayed to him, "Flight 58 delayed. There is no definite time of arrival". He was so worried that he went to the airlines desk and asked what was going on. They told him that the plane was circling over the storm waiting for it to settle down so they could land.

Kevin immediately started praying for Terri's plane to have a safe landing. The announcement came over the loud speaker, "Flight 58 is going to go to Minneapolis to wait out this storm. They might arrive later today or possibly tomorrow." Kevin immediately called his mom and told her what was going on "What should I do, I'm scared." His mom answered with, "Calm down, it will work out. Be patient and wait there at the airport and keep checking in at the airlines. Keep me informed." "Okay mom, thanks, will do."

After about two hours the storm had let up. He went outside and could still hear thunder rumbling in the far distance to the west and the sun was trying very hard to shine.

He went to the airline desk and found out that Terri's plane was about to arrive and should be landing safely in ninety minutes.

Kevin was so relieved and hoped that Terri wasn't too frightened. He tried to read a couple of magazines but they couldn't keep his interest. Then a lady asked him if he was waiting on flight 58. He told her yes and his girlfriend was on the plane. He was surprised that he called Terri his girlfriend when he actually had never thought of her that way. The lady said her daughter was on that flight and flying in from St. Louis for the holiday weekend. They chatted for awhile and then Kevin dismissed himself to get something to drink. He offered the lady if she would like him to bring something back for her. She declined so Kevin ventured on. He found a soft drink machine and luckily it had bottled water so that's what he got. Then he went looking for a restroom.

After leaving the restroom he checked the board and saw that flight 58 would be arriving in twenty minutes. He hurriedly went to the designated gate to wait for her. He kept checking his phone for the time and thought about calling his mom again but decided to wait until she arrived. It was about seven-thirty by then so he was thinking of a place in Des Moines to take Terri to dinner.

In that moment people started coming down the hall. He saw the lady that he had been talking to hugging her daughter. He was still waiting for Terri.

She saw him first and came running into his arms. He hugged her so tight that she could hardly breathe. He kissed her desperately.

She said, "I thought I was never going to get here. We had to fly to Minneapolis and sit on the plane for an hour and then we took off for here!"

He told her, "I know, I have been watching the monitor board and talking to the people at the airline desk. Were you scared?"

She told him that she was not scared. She was just put out about the inconvenience it was causing him. She then told Kevin that she wanted to call her mom and let her know that she had finally made it to Des Moines. Kevin told her he had to do the same.

They both called their moms. Kevin grabbed the carry on and they headed to the luggage area to get her suitcase. It was about twenty minutes and they were in his jeep. He asked if she was hungry and she told him that she was famished. He told her that he was too. "I'll take you to dinner and then we will head to Pella." Kevin announced. "Great" Terri said.

He drove to a small café that he had been to a couple of times. They went in and had a nice dinner and back talked a mile a minute. Then they were in the jeep and headed to Pella. He told her it would take almost an hour to get there. She told him that she was looking forward to meeting his parents and especially Cat.

Kevin told her that Cat wanted her to sleep in her room with her. However, you will have my room and I'll sleep in the basement in a makeshift bedroom.

She told him she was sorry to inconvenience him and he told her that he slept down there a lot in the summer because it was cooler.

They were talking nonstop and he turned off the interstate and said "here we are." She asked where the town was and he told her that he would show her tomorrow because his home was in the opposite direction. He made a couple turns here and there and pulled into his driveway. It was a three bedroom ranch and smaller than her house in St. Louis. He made some sort of an excuse for it and she said, "Don't worry about it."

Then Cat came running out to greet them. She didn't even acknowledge Kevin and ran to Terri and gave her a big hug. She said, "Hi, I'm Cat, come on in and see my room."

Kevin interrupted and said, "Hold on Cat, she needs to meet mom and dad first."

With that he saw his mom standing inside the front door and told Terri he would get her luggage later to come on in and meet his parents. His mom opened the door and Kevin made the introduction. She welcomed her to their home and invited her in to meet Kevin's dad. He was as mannerly as Kevin and Kevin looked just like him and he thought Cat looked just like her mother.

They visited for awhile and Kevin went out to his jeep to get Terri's things, brought them in and put them in his room where Terri would be staying. His parents offered Terri something cool to drink and she said water would be fine. Kevin then went to the kitchen and returned with a glass of ice water for Terri and one for him.

It was almost midnight by then and Kevin's dad said that he needed to hit the sack because he had to go to work in the morning. Kevin's mom said she needed to work tomorrow too and she asked, "Kevin, bring Terri by the store tomorrow." Kevin said he would. Cat went on to bed and Kevin showed Terri his room and they talked quietly for about ten minutes. Then he kissed her goodnight and headed for the basement.

Terri looked around the room and saw many signs of Kevin growing up. There were pictures, posters, plaques and trophies. She thought to herself how glad she was to be there. Then she put on her pajamas and went across the hall to brush her teeth. She was so tired that she went back to the bedroom and went to sleep in no time. She dreamed about Kevin all night.

The next morning Kevin woke up at nine-thirty. He couldn't believe what time it was. He hurriedly put the same clothes on that he wore the day before, went into the half bath next to where he slept, went to the bathroom, splashed water in his face, brushed his teeth and halfway ran a brush through his hair and hurriedly went upstairs.

Both Terri's and Cat's doors were closed to their bedrooms so he went to the kitchen to grab a cup of coffee and put the tea kettle on so he could make Terri hot tea.

Then he went and tapped quietly on Terri's door and heard a faint voice telling him to come in. He opened the door and she was still in bed and half asleep. He said, "Good morning darling." She opened her beautiful blue eyes widely and her dark hair was spilled all over the pillow. He said, "Are you ready to get up and see the town? I have water in the tea kettle if you want me to bring you some tea?" She answered with, "You are so sweet and I would love some tea."

With that he went to the kitchen, got the tea and returned. She was sitting on the side of the bed and looked beautiful. She told him thanks and after drinking a few sips of tea, said she would like to take a shower. She asked how she should dress. He told her shorts, t-shirt and sandals would be fine. With that he headed to his mom and dad's bedroom to shower and shave on put on the shorts he wore yesterday. Terri was still in the bathroom so he went in to get clean clothes and returned to his parent's room to dress. By then Terri was dressed herself and gave him a good morning kiss. He told her that they would be going into town for breakfast and then to see his mom's store and maybe out to his dad's job site later where he had been working.

Then he crashed into Cat's room and said, "Get up sleepy head. You and I have places to go and people to see and show off Terri." Cat was up, dressed and ready to go in ten minutes. They all piled in the jeep and headed into town for breakfast.

CHAPTER 25

First, Kevin drove around town and showed her the huge windmill and grandstand in the town square and he pointed out some of the Dutch architecture on the buildings. Then he parked on the square and said, "Here we are at my favorite place for breakfast." They went into the café and almost everyone there knew Kevin and Cat. Kevin introduced Terri to the owner who was at the register. A cute waitress about Kevin's age came up with three glasses of water and menus. Kevin told Terri, "This is my friend Becky. We went to high school together." Becky said she was glad to meet Terri and then walked off to take food to another table.

When Becky returned, Cat ordered pancakes. Kevin ordered sausage, eggs, hash browns and biscuits and gravy. Terri chose the ham and cheese omelet. In a very short time breakfast was on the table. Kevin kept telling Terri how glad he was that she was there. After breakfast he told Terri that he was taking her to the best Dutch bakery in the world for dessert. Cat told them that she would skip the bakery and go to her mom's store and would meet them there later.

Kevin and Terri took a walk for awhile and he pointed out some more of the Dutch architecture. They wandered a little off the square and he pointed out the dying tulips lining the streets of the neighborhood. He told her that they were the flowers from the tulip festival in the spring and told her that he really wanted her to see it in person sometime.

Kevin was so excited that Terri was there that he could not stop rambling on about the town.

Soon they were back at the town square and he took her into the bakery he had been talking about. Terri was overwhelmed at all the pastries and breads they had to offer. Her eyes glanced around and saw lots of Dutch painted plates, glassware and vases. Then Kevin nudged her and said, "See anything you want to try?" She noticed these large pastries shaped in an S form. She asked Kevin what they were. He answered, "Oh my favorite. They are called almond letters. They have a really flaky crust, almond extract filling and very lightly powdered with powdered sugar."

Terri asked, "Can we get one and share it?" He said "Sure."

So he ordered the almond letter to go. They next headed to a very small convenience store four doors away. He bought two half pints of milk. They walked across the street to sit on a bench facing the windmill. He could hardly wait for Terri to taste the pastry. He pulled out the milk and opened them and told her that you could not eat almond letters without milk.

She tasted the pastry and grinned and said, "This is absolutely the best pastry I have ever had. Maybe we could come here Tuesday morning before you take me to the airport and I could get some to take home?" Kevin told her that they sure could.

Terri began to tell him how much he looked like his dad and that Cat looked exactly like her mom. Kevin answered, "Yes my dad is a good looking fella."

Terri laughed and continued enjoying the almond letter.

When they were finished they walked over to his mom's store. She had several people shopping so he went to the register to start checking people out. He told Terri to go ahead and look around. Cat was even waiting on customers. Soon his mom walked up and thanked him for helping out at the register. He said, "No problem." She asked him where Terri was and he told her she was somewhere in the store. Kevin's mom went looking for Terri.

When she found her, she gave her a quick hug and welcomed her to the store. Terri told her how much she was enjoying looking around and that she especially liked the handmade Dutch items. She told Kevin's mom how unique they were and so different from most gift shops she had been in.

Then Terri walked up with three items. She told Kevin that she was buying them for her mom and two aunts so they would have original Dutch made items.

Kevin told her, "You are family so you get fifty percent off." Terri told him, "No, I will pay full price." Then Kevin responded with, "Oh no you won't madam."

Terri chuckled at that and paid half price and Kevin carefully wrapped the items, put them in a box and taped them shut. He told Terri she could take the box as a carry on with her other small bag.

Soon his mom came back up front and told Kevin that he and Terri could leave because the store had slowed down. He asked his mom if she wanted him to take Cat with them.

His mom said no that she may need her there. Cat was always a big help to her mom and the business.

Kevin and Terri left and then walked around for awhile. Kevin pointed out the Old Dutch architecture of the buildings. There was an old three story hotel and he took her inside to see the lobby. It was all antique furniture and fixtures and an area rug in the middle with a windmill in the middle and lots of tulips around it.

Terri was fascinated with the hotel lobby. Kevin told her that they rarely rent rooms to tourist except for the tulip festival in the spring. The top floor was rented monthly to people and there were only eight rooms on the second floor to rent to guests.

Then they left the hotel and soon were back at Kevin's jeep. He said, "Let's go to my dad's job site and I will show you where I have been working for most of the summer." He told her it was about four miles north of town and she would see lots of cornfields and soy beans.

Terri was amazed at all the crops and how flat Iowa was compared to Missouri. They passed a few farms with two story white houses, a barn, a shed nearby and the only place she saw trees was shading the farm houses.

Pretty soon Kevin turned into a lane and saw his dad and crew working on a huge barn. When they pulled up his dad greeted them, gave Terri a hug and asked, "What have you two been up to?" Kevin filled him in on their morning. He told Terri that he and another crew member were going to start painting it next week. "Come on, I will introduce you to Jeff."

Jeff was a high school dropout and had worked for Ruble Construction ever since. Kevin's dad had convinced him to get his GED and Jeff did.

After meeting Jeff they said goodbye to the crew and his dad. He told his dad that he would have dinner ready when he got home.

When they got back in the jeep and were heading for town Terri asked Kevin if he liked to cook. He told her he loved to grill but tonight he was making a meatloaf, baked sweet potatoes and some fresh green beans and tomatoes from the neighbor's garden.

"How does that sound?" he asked and Terri quickly answered, "Yummy, especially because you are making it."

Kevin confessed that his mom had a very good meatloaf recipe so he would definitely be following it.

When they entered town Kevin stopped at a very small gas station and filled up with gas. He went inside to pay and Terri noticed the pumps were old and did not have pay at the pump options like she was used to in St. Louis.

Kevin returned with a coke for her and an iced tea for him. He told her they didn't have lemon there so he would drink his tea without.

He drove her around for awhile and showed her where he went to school. The entire school was in one location. Terri saw this as very different. She didn't think there was a school in St. Louis where you could go kindergarten through twelfth grade all in one location.

Then they headed back to Kevin's house. It was a magnificent day so they went to sit on the patio to finish their drinks.

Kevin leaned over and kissed Terri and asked if she was having a good time. Terri answered, "The best and thank you for showing me around." Then he kissed her again and told her she was welcome and thanked her for coming.

He had mixed up the meatloaf and tightly packed it into a loaf pan and had drizzled ketchup over the top. The sweet potatoes were wrapped in foil and he put them and the meatloaf in the oven and set a timer for one hour.

He then told Terri that when the beans started to boil he would turn them down and let them simmer until dinner. He looked in the pantry and saw a loaf of French bread. He took it out of the package, got some foil out and put the other half back in the pantry. He put the bread on a cutting board and sliced it. He carefully buttered and garlic powdered the slices of bread then he put it back together as a loaf and wrapped it in foil. "I'll put this in the oven about fifteen minutes before we eat."

Terri was so amazed at his knowledge of cooking. She asked him how he learned to cook and he told her mostly by trial and error. With both his parents working he learned very young so he could help his mother out.

Terri thought about her lifestyle at home. Her parents always cooked on weekends and they usually had enough left overs until Tuesday or Wednesday. Then her dad would stop and bring carryout home for dinner or her mom would drive through Kentucky Fried Chicken and bring it for dinner. However in a small town like Pella most people cooked because there were not a lot of places for carry out.

His mom and Cat got home first and Cat enticed Terri to come to her room so she could show off her stuff. Kevin and his mom sat in the kitchen and visited. Kevin got up, poured his mom a glass of wine and spoke, "You look like you need this." She answered, "You are reading my mind."

Kevin had made tea for himself and instant lemonade for Cat. About half way through the wine she called for Cat to come set the table. Terri offered to help her so the two of them quickly set the table.

Kevin's dad walked in sweaty and dirty. He said he didn't want to delay dinner but he wanted to take a shower first and his wife told him to go ahead, there was time.

Mr. Ruble returned in shorts, t-shirt and flip flops and announced that he felt better and was ready to eat.

Kevin jumped up and took things from the oven. He put the bread in a long basket but left the foil on. He sliced the meatloaf and put it on the table. He unwrapped the sweet potatoes and put one on each plate. Cat had already put butter, salt and pepper on when she set the table. He got out a plate of fresh tomatoes that he had sliced and put on the table. He then grabbed a couple oven mittens and put the steaming pot of green beans in the middle of the table on an oven pad. Cat had already taken drink orders and had them on the table. Kevin put a salad bowl by each plate and told Terri that it was for the beans. He then opened the bread and everyone helped themselves. He ladled Terri some beans as well as himself. His mom and dad complimented him on how good everything was.

Terri ate everything on her plate and thought it was wonderful. She even picked up the salad bowl and drank the juice from the beans. She saw Cat doing it so she followed.

Kevin laughed and said, "You are becoming a real Iowa girl instead of a city slicker." His parents chuckled at that.

After dinner his mom told Kevin for him and Terri to go do something that she and Cat would do the dishes. Mr. Ruble settled in his chair in the living room and turned on the television to catch the news.

Kevin and Terri headed for the basement to play video games. When they got down there Kevin took her in his arms and kissed her. She was delighted.

CHAPTER 26

The next day they had both slept until ten or so. Terri woke up, took a shower and washed her hair. Kevin appeared, tapped on the door and said, "Can I come in?" Terri answered with, "I guess so but I am only wearing a towel." He said, "Great" and entered the bathroom and watched her finish drying her hair. Then he took her into his arms, hugged her and gave her a good morning kiss. When she backed away the towel had slipped and her breasts were exposed. Kevin thought he was going to faint. She quickly turned and pulled up the towel and told him, "I had better get out of here, I am so embarrassed." Kevin's response was, "Don't be because I loved it" and then he winked at her.

She quickly went into the bedroom to dress. Kevin took a quick shower and shaved. He wrapped a towel around him to get dressed but Terri was still in his room where his clothes were. He tapped on the door and she told him to come in. She was dressed and said she would be in the kitchen. He hurriedly dressed and went to the kitchen.

She had a puzzled look on her face. She finally said, "I can't believe that you saw my breasts." Kevin reassured her that it was an accident and to please not worry about it. However he was thinking to himself how magnificent they looked and could not stop thinking about it. The subject was dropped.

His mom had left for the store and his dad went to help their church set up the soft drinks booth. Cat went with her mother to help in the store.

Kevin asked if she wanted some breakfast. She asked if he had any cereal and that would be sufficient. Kevin went to the pantry and got three boxes of cereal. Then he got milk from the refrigerator, two bowls and spoons. He poured them both a glass of orange juice and joined Terri at the table.

She chose her cereal and Kevin chose the same one. They munched on the cereal and not much conversation happened. Kevin started off with their plans for the day. He told her that most of the town and surrounding farmers would all show up at the town square to celebrate the fourth. He told her there would be entertainment on the grand stand most of the day and there would be several food and drink booths set up around in different areas. He said the churches frowned on selling beer so the city hasn't allowed a beer booth for the past three years. He said it is really pretty fun. "Are you ready for it Terri?" he asked. She told him, "Of course, it sounds fun like a small version of the VP fair at the arch in St. Louis. Will there be fireworks tonight?"

He answered, "Well of course. Only everyone goes to the high school football field and sit in the bleachers to see the fireworks display."

They had finished their cereal and juice when Terri jumped up and rinsed the bowls and placed them in the dishwasher. Kevin put the milk and cereal away. Then they jumped in his jeep and headed for the town square.

He couldn't find a place to park so he pulled into the alley behind his mom's store. He parked behind his mom's car and his dad's truck. They went in the back door at the store. His mom said, "Thank goodness you are here. Cat and I are swamped. Can you handle the register for awhile?" He told his mom, "Sure, no problem." Then he looked at Terri and she nodded her approval. Terri went to the register with him and packaged up merchandise that was purchased. She thought it was fun. Kevin introduced her to about half the people as his friend from St. Louis. He didn't have to dwell on the subject because there was a line at the register. He leaned over and told her that by noon they would be done because everyone went to see the entertainment on the stage. He told her that the high school band started it off and played mostly patriotic songs. They would stop and everyone would stand and say the pledge of allegiance to the flag.

Terri thought it was cool and she was anxious to participate.

As Kevin had told her, it had slowed down by eleven thirty. His mom told Kevin, Terri and Cat to go join the festivities. Cat ran off to be with her friends. Kevin and Terri found a spot in the grass and sat down.

The band was in place on the grandstand. Right at noon the drummer did a drum roll and a loud siren went off that could be heard miles around. Then the band played three numbers. The director announced, "Now please stand and say the pledge of allegiance."

Everyone stood up, faced the flag and said the pledge. Then the band continued until about ten.

He said to Terri that it would be awhile before the next entertainment started and suggested they get something to eat. He took her by the fireman's fish and chip booth. He told Terri that was what he was getting and asked what she wanted. As he went to order their lunch he gave her a ten dollar bill and asked her to go to the next booth and get three cokes. He told her that he was taking lunch to his mom. He told her that his dad would be working in the booth. It was sponsored by their church. She did as told and Kevin got three orders of fish and chips. The chips were actually sliced potatoes and deep fried. He grabbed some packets of tartar sauce and ketchup and stuffed them in his pockets. He grabbed a handful of napkins and turned around to find Terri standing there with three cokes in a carrying tray. They headed to his mom's store. There was a cute bench in front. He put the food down, got his mom's lunch and took one of the cokes. He told Terri to sit on the bench and he would be right back. He took lunch in to his mom and she thanked him and then he went back outside to eat with Terri. As they began to eat his friend Craig walked up with his wife, Karen. She was a very pretty, petite black woman, maybe eighteen and wore her hair in a short afro style. Kevin quickly stood up, gave Karen a hug and introduced her to Terri. They visited a short while and Craig said he was starving and they were headed to the food booth and would see them later.

Terri asked Kevin, "I haven't seen but a few black people here." Kevin answered her that they were definitely a minority in Pella. He told her that he and Craig became friends in eighth grade and they have been best friends ever since.

They sat at the bench enjoying their lunch. Terri complimented him on their choice. She told him how good the sandwich was and especially how yummy the chips were.

Several people walked by and probably half of them said hello to Kevin and he answered them all by saying their names and returning the greeting. Terri told him, "This is so cool how you know all these people. I don't even know all my neighbors' names." Kevin laughed at that comment and said, "Well that's the way it is in a small town." She smiled.

Around two a country band started entertaining and a lot of people had gathered around. Some folks were even dancing on the concrete slab in front of the grandstand. Terri asked, "What kind of dance is that?" Kevin almost busted out laughing and told her, "It is called the Texas Two Step." She admitted she had never seen it.

They went into his mom's store to throw away their trash. His mom told him to go have fun because she was fine by herself. There were only a few people coming in once in a while and not many buying. So Kevin and Terri ventured out into the square. He asked if she wanted to get an almond letter and she told him that she was stuffed but maybe later she would have room to split one.

They walked around and saw a lot of the game booths. He played a dart game and won a miniature set of Dutch wooden shoes. He gave them to Terri and said, "Here is a souvenir for you." They were on a long red and blue ribbon and he put them around her neck. She leaned up and kissed him on the cheek and thanked him. He then said, "Now you are a real Dutch girl." He couldn't help but laugh out loud.

Kevin told her that he wanted to go back and help his mom out at the store so she could have a break. Terri told him, "That would be great."

His mom was glad to see them and headed back to the break room to sit down and relax. She had put several items at half price by the register. When she returned thirty minutes later, Kevin had sold almost three-quarters of the items at half price and Terri had carefully wrapped the items and packaged them so they wouldn't get broken. His mom told them they had better head to the grandstand because the rock and roll band started at five and Jennifer would be looking for him. He told his mom that he hadn't run into her yet but Kevin's mom told him that she was there because she was in the store asking about him.

They walked outside and Terri asked, "Who is Jennifer, an old girlfriend?" Kevin snorted and answered, "No hardly. She was my dance partner in high school. We never dated or were at all romantic. All we did was dance. She was elected best dancer in our class along with me. Our picture is even in my senior yearbook. Don't worry Terri, no romance there, just friends and dancing."

They walked over to the grandstand and the rock and roll band had just started playing. Kevin said, "Come on, let's dance and show this town what a good dancer you are." Some people applauded when the song was over and they returned to a spot in the grass. The band played a couple more songs and Terri heard Kevin singing along. She said, "You have a nice voice." He just laughed.

About that time, the band announced they were playing "September by Earth, Wind and Fire." It was his and Jennifer's favorite dance number. They had even made a routine to that song. In an instant, Jennifer showed up and grabbed Kevin's hand and said, "Let's go bub." He looked at Terri and she signaled him to go ahead. She could hardly believe her eyes when she watched them dancing. He even flipped her over his shoulder. People crowded around to watch them.

Terri sat there in amazement. It was like watching professional dancers. The song came to an end and people were cheering, "Go Kevin, go Jennifer." He and Jennifer came back to where Terri was standing.

Kevin quickly said, "Jennifer this is my girlfriend from St. Louis and Terri this is Jennifer." Terri was elated that he introduced her as his girlfriend. He had always introduced her before as my friend from St. Louis. Terri told Jennifer that she was so glad to meet her and complimented her on her dance skills. Jennifer answered back, "Yes, Kevin and I practiced on that routine for a month before we ever showed it to anyone."

Before another word was said, Kevin's friends Craig and Karen showed up and hugged Kevin and Jennifer and told them that they still had it. Later Kevin credited his mom and grandmother for his dance skills. When he was a kid and spending time at his grandma's she was always dancing around the kitchen and pretending that a kitchen chair was her partner. Before Kevin knew it, he was the kitchen chair and learning all her steps.

Terri thought that is was a great story and how lucky he was to have a grandmother that was so much fun.

The band finished at six. The major came to the microphone to award prizes for the best decorated store front. The hotel was first, Kevin's mom second and the bakery third. Kevin's mom got a small trophy and twenty five dollars. She spent way more than that to decorate but was happy for second place. The hotel always was first since Kevin could remember.

After the awards a group of people came on stage, all wearing Dutch costumes and wooden shoes. They sang a couple songs and then the drummer and banjos started playing. All the people in costumes did some sort of Dutch dance. Terri couldn't believe they could dance that way in those wooden shoes.

When they finished, the crowd started thinning out. It was seven thirty by then. People left to get some supper and head to the high school for the fireworks at the stadium.

Kevin and Terri went and got an almond letter before the bakery closed. They bought the last one. They walked across the street, sat on a bench and shared the pastry. Terri remarked, "What a day. This is great." Kevin responded by leaning over and giving her a kiss.

They returned to his mom's shop and it was closed. All the food booths were shutting down. They walked around the block to the alley where the jeep was parked. He noticed the back door to the shop was open. He could see his mom and dad. His dad said, "We have been waiting for you to move your jeep so we could leave." They told him that they were headed home for a bite to eat and Kevin told them that he and Terri would join them. Cat rode home with them in the jeep.

They arrived at Kevin's house. His mom pulled out deli ham, cheese and chips. She put out paper plates. Kevin poured himself a glass of milk, Cat and Terri wanted lemonade. They all made their own sandwiches and ate on the patio. After dinner Cat cleared the table and was anxious to get to the football stadium to be with her friends. Kevin grabbed a blanket and headed off for the stadium with both Terri and Cat. Cat ran off to find her friends and Kevin and Terri found a spot on the lawn to spread out the blanket and in good view of where the fireworks would go off. The high school band was performing on the field. The stadium was practically full. Soon Craig showed up, found Terri and Kevin and spread out their own blanket. It was starting to get dark and the band was marching off.

Then an extremely loud boom went off and the fireworks began. There were small ones at first for thirty minutes. As it got darker the magnificent ones started. Terri leaned over and told Kevin how much fun she was having. Then several big ones went off followed by the finale.

Kevin, Terri and his parents took their time leaving. Kevin told his mom that he had told Cat to meet him at his jeep because she knew where they parked.

They all drove back to Kevin's house. After going inside his mom announced that grandma and Aunt Donna were driving down from Fort Dodge in the morning to spend the day. Cat was excited. Kevin told Terri she was going to meet his grandma the next day and that he thought the world of his Aunt Donna. Her thirty years of marriage ended in divorce, and had no kids; about four years ago she convinced his grandma to move in with her at Fort Dodge. Actually he told Terri that it had worked and very well. His grandma joined a senior citizen dance club and she was very happy there.

It had been a long and busy day so by eleven thirty everyone was headed for bed. Kevin kissed Terri and told her that he would see her in the morning.

CHAPTER 27

They all awoke early to prepare for grandma. They had barely finished breakfast, done the dishes and Mrs. Ruble took a bag of frozen chicken breast out of the freezer to thaw. Grandma Caroline and his Aunt were ringing the front doorbell.

Cat ran to answer the door and give her grandma, whom she was named after, and her aunt big hugs and kisses. She escorted them into the kitchen and the whole family affectionately greeted their guests. Then Kevin took Terri's hand and said, "Terri, this is my grandma Catherine that I have told you about and my Aunt Donna."

Grandma instantly gave Terri a hug and said, "So glad to meet you." Then Terri shook hands with Aunt Donna and all was well.

Cat took over the conversation and grandma and Aunt Donna paid close attention. She told them about the wonderful summer she had been having and also told them about her dance recital and her jazz solo.

Grandma told her that she wanted to see it. Cat ran to her room to put on her costumes and get the CD with the music.

Terri commented, "I have been waiting to see this." Kevin came back with, "It's really good."

In fifteen minutes Cat appeared with her jazz dress shoes on. She put a CD in the player and everyone went to the living room to watch her perform. The dance took about fifteen minutes and when she was finished, Terri ran over, gave her a hug and said, "That was absolutely wonderful." Grandma and Aunt Donna did the same.

Kevin's mom asked if anyone was ready for coffee. Grandma said, "I thought you would never ask." Everyone else sat and visited while Mrs. Ruble was getting the coffee. Cat returned back to her room to put her shorts and t-shirt back on. She came out with white shorts and a maroon t-shirt that Kevin had given her from Missouri State with the college logo on it. Kevin smiled and said, "Looks good Cat." Terri announced that she needed one of those shirts.

Grandma announced, "What time is lunch, we probably need to leave by five." Aunt Helen said, "Settle down mom. We will leave whenever, we have no time schedule."

It was noon by then so Kevin's mom went to the kitchen to do some prep work for lunch and Kevin went to help.

His mom asked, "Do you think Terri will be okay in there with grandma?" He answered, "Don't worry mom, Terri can hold her own."

Before long Kevin found himself outside grilling the chicken and Terri joined him. She told Kevin how much she liked his grandma. Kevin's mom had made a salad and was roasting fresh vegetables in the oven. She also wrapped fresh asparagus in bacon and brought them out to Kevin to grill.

Twenty minutes later his mom came to the patio door and asked Kevin how long until the grilled food was ready. Kevin told her about ten minutes.

Cat had the table set inside. Kevin put the chicken on one platter and the asparagus on another. They took it to the table and Kevin put a chicken breast on everyone's plate. He set the asparagus platter on the table. Grandma insisted that she say grace so they all bowed their heads and when grandma finally said amen, they all repeated and began to eat.

They all talked about the weather. Grandma inquired about Kevin's grades and where Terri went to college. Terri explained that she had just graduated high school and was hoping to start Drury in the fall. Kevin told his grandma that Drury was in Springfield where he went to Missouri State. Grandma had no comment.

Five o' clock came and grandma and Aunt Helen took off for Fort Dodge. Kevin's mom was exhausted by then. She told everyone that she was going to lay down for a bit. His dad headed to the living room to watch television and Cat headed off to her room to call her friend.

Kevin told Terri, "Let's go for a drive so we can be alone." Terri agreed and out the door they went. Terri asked, "Where are we going?" Kevin answered, "I think we will take a ride out to the lake and go for a walk." She told him that it would be great to spend time alone with him since it was her last night there. Kevin agreed.

They arrived at the lake and got out of the jeep. Kevin had bought some old bread so they could feed the ducks. They went to a small dock and the ducks came from all direction to greet them. They were the only two people at the lake.

Terri threw bread crumbs to the ducks and had fun doing it. Then they walked the perimeter of the lake. By then it was going on eight. After that they sat on a bench facing west. The sun was going down with a perfect clear sky. He said, "I think we will just sit here and watch the sun set. It should be magnificent tonight." With that, he reached over, put his arms around her and kissed her with much passion. He even surprised himself, let alone Terri.

Terri remarked, "Where did that come from?" He then leaned in close and stated, "Terri, I know it is early in our relationship but I am falling in love with you. You are like someone I have never known. Even the very first time I saw you on the beach, I was so impressed. I am so glad that after my run we met up again and things went from there."

Terri sat silent for a few minutes and then kissed Kevin and said, "I am extremely fond of you and care a great deal for you but love is a pretty solid word in my book. Are you sure about what you just said?" He then told her that he was sure he was and wanted her to feel the same about him.

Time had passed and the sun was beginning to set. It was absolutely beautiful. Terri got her camera out of her purse and took some pictures. The reflection on the lake was magnificent. Then she took a picture of Kevin.

He got his phone out and took pictures of her too. Then they huddled together and took a few selfies on both cameras. Then they started laughing about it and began kissing and cuddling.

At about ten, Kevin said, "We better go; we will stop and get something to eat in town." So they walked back to the jeep but before he started the engine, he leaned over and kissed her again.

They stopped and got a burger and soft drinks in town and ate in the jeep. They talked a long time about her going to Drury, if her dad agreed and how much fun they would have in Springfield the next school year.

By then it was eleven thirty and Kevin said that they had better go home and get some sleep. They had to leave at ten to head to Des Moines to get her flight at noon.

He kissed her goodnight before they went into the house and again when he walked her to her room. Then he went to the basement to hit the sack. It took him a long time to fall asleep because all he could think about was Terri and that she was leaving the next day.

Terri awoke very early around six thirty. She hurried and took a shower and dressed. By seven fifteen she headed for the kitchen. Kevin's parents were at the table drinking coffee. Mr. Ruble had just finished a bowl of cereal and was about ready to leave for work.

Terri walked in and said good morning, got herself a cup of coffee and joined them. She said, "I am glad I caught the two of you before you left for work. I really want to thank you for having me this weekend. I really enjoyed being here, all the activities and your hospitality."

Mrs. Ruble stood up, went to Terri, hugged her and said, "You are very welcome and I have suspicions that our son has some pretty strong feelings for you."

Mr. Ruble decided to stay out of the conversation, got up and kissed his wife, hugged Terri and told her, "Sure hope you come back sometime. We enjoyed having you." Then out the back door he went heading for the job site.

About eight thirty, Kevin came up the stairs and was surprised to see Terri and his mom having coffee and visiting. He said, "Good morning and now I am headed for the shower." It only took him twenty minutes or so to shower, shave, get dressed and return to the kitchen. His mom was preparing French toast and asked Kevin to go wake up Cat. She wanted to take Cat to work for awhile before she headed to the pool with her friends.

So Cat dragged herself out of bed and joined them for breakfast. Her mom told her to pack her swimsuit in her bag. She wanted Cat to help straighten up the shelves and refill merchandise. After such a busy weekend it needed it.

Mrs. Ruble and Cat left at nine and Kevin and Terri cleaned up the kitchen. Terri told him that she needed to pack her suitcase. He followed her into the room and watched her pack and they were trying to figure out the next time they would see each other.

When she finished, she said, "Let's load up and get going. I would like to stop by Craig's store to say goodbye." Kevin told her that Craig would love that.

They loaded up and headed to Craig's store. He said, "I am surprised to see you guys." Kevin responded, "Terri wanted to say goodbye." Craig was very pleased. Terri gave him a hug and told him how nice it was to meet Kevin's best friend and sent her regards to his wife.

All goodbyes were done and they were on their way to the airport in Des Moines. Kevin stopped for gas and in about an hour they were at the airport, checked in her luggage and walked to where she was to load the plane. They had thirty minutes or so before she loaded so they sat in a very crowded waiting area. They talked for awhile and Kevin asked her who was picking her up at the airport in St. Louis. She answered her dad because he was off a couple months from the University. She told Kevin that he would probably play golf most days.

The time came for Terri to load the plane. Kevin almost teary eyed walked with her as far as he could, put his arms around her and kissed her. She hugged him back and then had to turn to go to the plane. He watched her and before she was out of sight she turned, threw him a kiss and mouthed the words, "I love you."

CHAPTER 28

Kevin drove back to Pella and all he could think about was Terri and the words she had mouthed to him before boarding the plane. He arrived home and couldn't wait for Terri's call that she was safe and sound in St. Louis.

Terri's plane took off on time and was almost to St. Louis when the pilot announced they were headed to Chicago because of very severe storms and hail in St. Louis. In thirty minutes her plane landed in Chicago. The plane unloaded everyone because the storm was headed for Chicago. She went to the waiting area and in thirty minutes they were told there would be no flights to St. Louis until the next morning. Terri went to a pay phone and called her mom to tell her what was going on.

Her mom said, "I don't want you sleeping in the airport." I'll call your great aunt Rita and you can take a cab to her house. Call me back in thirty minutes and I'll fill you in on what to do.

She called her mom back and was told to take a cab to Aunt Rita's. Terri wrote down the address and phone number. She went to an ATM and got cash for the cab. She got her suitcases and walked out where she could take a cab.

A cab picked her up and off she went to Aunt Rita's. The cab driver told her he was sorry but he had to stop at a gas station to use the restroom. He parked on the side and went into the men's room. Terri was reading a magazine and when the cab started up and drove off, she assumed it was the cab driver, but it wasn't. The man stole the cab with Terri in it and took off at a high speed and swerved in and out of traffic before she noticed it wasn't the cab driver. She said, "What are you doing, please slow down." He responded for her to shut up and she wouldn't get hurt.

After winding around about in what looked to be a warehouse region, he finally pulled up in front of a large black door, got out, opened the door and pulled in to a very large warehouse. He took the cab key and cab radio and left her there in the dark. He ran outside and closed the huge black door. Terri sat there alone in the dark and started to cry. She noticed that the cab radio was still working because the cab company kept calling it but she had no microphone to answer it.

She got out of the car and saw a side door and went outside hoping to find a pay phone. She was surrounded by tall warehouse buildings and walked around a couple of blocks and no pay phone was anywhere in sight. She went back to the garage where the cab was and went in the side door. She then decided to open the big garage door so she would have more light. She saw the microphone and the floor and picked it up and got back in the cab and started honking the horn but no one showed up.

In the meantime the original cab driver had reported that his cab had been stolen with his passenger. The police came and he told them the passenger was a young female around twenty. He remembered where he was supposed to take her. It was an easy address to remember. He told the police it was "33 West 333rd street".

The police looked up the address and found a Rita Moon lived there and gave her a phone call. They told her what had happened and she told them that she was her great aunt and was wondering why she hadn't arrived. It had been two hours since she had called and said she was taking a taxi to her house.

The police told Aunt Rita that they would keep her informed. Rita immediately called Terri's mom and told her what was happening. Terri's mom was panicked and called her husband to tell him. They decided that she would drive to Chicago to be with Aunt Rita and he would stay home in case of any news.

Within thirty minutes, Terri's mom was on the highway headed to Chicago. She called the Chicago police two times on the way to see if her daughter had been found and both times she had not.

CHAPTER 29

Terri saw the microphone to the radio on the garage floor and picked it up and went back to the cab. She was trying to figure out how to hook it back up but had no idea how. She started crying again and could hardly get a hold of herself.

She kept thinking If only I had a cell phone. So she would buy one herself if her parents wouldn't.

Terri's mom arrived at Aunt Rita's and no word yet. They both broke down in tears.

Terri examined the microphone and where to hook it up. She found a pocket knife and screw driver in the glove box in the cab. She examined the wiring and started trying to figure out how to rewire it. She knew that if Kevin was there that he would know how to do it. After thirty minutes she gave up and just sat there in the cab and cried.

She and Kevin must have been sending vibes to each other. It had been almost eight hours since Terri left and he hadn't heard from her. He called her mom's cell phone and she told him what had happened and Terri had been kidnapped. Kevin panicked and then began packing a duffle bag. He told his parents he was driving to Chicago to find Terri. His mom tried to stop him but he was determined and left in his jeep for Chicago.

The police went to the address where Aunt Rita lived but she hadn't heard a word from Terri. When Terri's mom arrived at Aunt Rita's house the police were still there. She was told that the kidnapper had robbed the gas station where her daughter had been kidnapped. There was a surveillance video of the robbery and the police were trying to identify him but hadn't yet.

Terri's mom was in tears and so was Aunt Rita. Kevin called again and Terri's mom answered. He was about an hour from Chicago and wanted to know an address where he could meet her. She gave him Aunt Rita's address and said she would see him soon.

CHAPTER 30

Terri got ahold of herself and walked to the door and opened it. She was definitely in a warehouse district. All the buildings were tall and grey. The doorway led to an alley so she tried to find a main street but had no luck. So she went back to the garage and sat in the cab but left the big garage door open for light.

She was glad that she had bought a candy bar and a bottle of water at the airport so she knew she would survive hunger or thirst.

She turned the lights on flashing in the cab and was hoping someone would notice the lights flashing from the open garage door.

She began to cry again and locked herself in the cab even though it was a hot afternoon. She ate one bite of the candy and drank a couple swallows of water.

An hour went by and she thought she heard a voice hollering. She slumped down in the seat and tried to peek out to find the voice that she had heard.

There was a tall lanky man standing in the open doorway of the garage. She hoped she could trust him and he would help her. Then she got out of the cab and yelled for help. The man came running over and asked what was going on. Terri was almost hysterical at that point and could hardly talk. She took a long hard swallow and explained to the man what had happened. He tried to calm her down but he couldn't until he pulled out his cell phone and said he was dialing 911.

The man's name was Peter and he lived in a loft about four blocks away and was out jogging when he saw the garage door open and the flashing lights from the cab.

Terri instantly calmed down when he told 911 their location and something suspicious was going on and asked for the police to come.

In five minutes they heard sirens coming and Terri was so relieved that she was standing next to Peter and holding on to him for dear life.

When the police arrived they asked both of them what was going on. Peter had no idea but Terri quickly informed them what had happened. They called their dispatch and got the story about the robber stealing that cab with a hostage inside.

The police notified the department that they had found the cab and the girl was alright. The two police asked Terri to go with them. She hesitated and asked Peter for his last name and cell phone number. He gave her his business card and also gave one to the police.

Terri's mom was instantly notified and by that time Kevin was with her and Aunt Rita. The three of them jumped in the car and followed the police to the station. They got out of the car and ran into the police station and there was Terri and she was trembling.

Her mom went to her first and practically suffocated her with hugs. Kevin moved in and told her how scared he was.

Terri's dad was on his way to Chicago but hadn't arrived yet. Her mom called him and told him that they had found her and she was okay but a little shaken up.

The police got all the information they needed to and then took Terri back to Aunt Rita's house. When they got there, Kevin took Terri in his arms and told her how much he loved her. He also said that he could not live without her.

Kevin called his mom to let her know that Terri had been found unharmed and that she was doing okay. She was glad to hear it because she had even closed her store and was thinking of driving to Chicago. Kevin's dad was home when he called and they both broke down in tears as well as Cat because they had told her what had happened.

CHAPTER 31

After about an hour or so, they were all rather settled down and Terri's dad came charging in the front door at Aunt Rita's. When Terri saw him she burst into tears again and he held her tightly and told her how scared he was and that he loved her with all his heart.

After awhile they all were somewhat settled down and Terri said she was hungry. So Aunt Rita ordered carry out from a nearby deli and they all almost devoured the food.

It was getting late by then and Aunt Rita had two guest rooms, one for Terri's parents, one for Terri and Kevin slept on the couch.

The next morning Aunt Rita fixed breakfast. The police called and said they had the kidnapper in custody and wanted Terri to identify him. Her dad took her to the police station and she identified the kidnapper.

All Terri wanted by then was some alone time with Kevin and her parents understood.

Kevin and Terri went for a long drive in his jeep and stopped several times to kiss and hug each other.

Terri told Kevin that if her dad wouldn't get her a cell phone that she would get one on her own. Kevin told her that he would pay for it.

When they got back to Aunt Rita's her folks were packing up to go home. Kevin looked so sad but he knew he had to say goodbye to her again.

They all piled into their own vehicles and headed in their own direction. But before they left, Kevin took Terri in his arms and kissed her passionately in front of her parents. He told her he loved her with all his being.

Her parents grinned and didn't seem surprised.

CHAPTER 32

Terri rode back to St. Louis with her dad. She wanted to talk to him about getting her a cell phone and allowing her to go to Drury.

Her dad told her not to worry because he was getting her a cell phone the next day. He also had been looking into Drury and so far he was very impressed. Terri knew her parents could afford it and also thought she could apply for scholarships.

Kevin finally arrived home in Pella about one in the morning. His mom was waiting for him. He was glad that she was. He wanted to talk to her about how much he cared for Terri. Everything he told her did not surprise his mom. She had already figured out how he loved Terri and so had Kevin's dad. She fixed him a sandwich and told him to get to bed because he was supposed to work for his dad the next day.

Before he went to bed, he called Terri on her landline and she answered on the second ring. He was glad she was home and told her he loved her and that he hated being so far away from her. Terri responded that she felt the same way. Then she told him that she would call him on her very own cell phone the next day because she and her dad were going in the morning to get one. Kevin was extremely happy to hear that. He told her he loved her again and said he was looking forward to be called the next day. He lay in bed, closed his eyes and dreamed of Terri all night. His dad let him sleep in the next morning until Cat came in to see him. He looked at the clock and it was already ten. He jumped up and told Cat that he had to get to work. She told him that their dad had let him sleep in and had told her to wake him up at ten. He hurried, got dressed, grabbed a cookie and glass of milk and headed out the door after kissing Cat goodbye.

When he arrived at the job site to work with his dad, his cell phone rang and it was an unknown number. He knew the area code was a Missouri number and answered it promptly. It was Terri and he was delighted. It was only ten thirty and she had her own phone. They talked for a couple of minutes and told each other how much they loved each other. Then they hung up. Kevin felt like he was already late for work. He immediately put Terri's number in his address book on his phone.

They talked two times a day the rest of the summer. One of her phone calls to Kevin was so exciting for both of them. Terri told him that she had gotten a scholarship to Drury and her dad had finally agreed to let her go there. They were both so excited that they could hardly stand it.

Terri had to be at Drury a week sooner than Kevin had to be at Missouri State. Her parents moved her in her dorm. She had her car too. They spent the night at a hotel, took Terri to breakfast the next day and then said their goodbyes. Terri's dad cried more than her mom on the way home.

Terri went through orientation and got registered for her classes. She was taking eighteen hours which was a big load for a first semester freshmen. She had decided to major in education and wanted to be a teacher.

Kevin went back to Missouri State the next week, moved in his dorm and immediately drove over to Drury to see Terri. She was waiting on the porch of her dorm for him. They ran into each other's arms, kissed, hugged, and kissed some more.

Classes were going to start the next day. Kevin was already registered for eighteen hours himself. It would be a busy semester. Since Kevin had changed his major to mechanical engineering, he was going to have to spend a great deal of time studying. It wasn't the easiest of majors.

Terri instantly fell in love with Drury and really liked her classes. She and Kevin agreed to only see each other one time between weekends. However, sometimes he showed up more just to give her a kiss and tell her how much he loved her. Terri was so pleased.

Every weekend they spent as much time as possible together. Even studying together but Kevin had a hard time studying with Terri at his side so he would stay up every night to catch up on his studies.

Kevin took Terri to his homecoming. They went to the parade, football game and dance. They loved dancing with each other. Drury didn't have a football team so they would not have homecoming until basketball season.

On several of their dates, Kevin was anxious to have sex with her but he held back out of respect for her and their beliefs. Terri wasn't pushing it either. She could wait until the time was right.

CHAPTER 33

The first semester flew by. Terri was loving college and seeing Kevin whenever she could. All of a sudden it was time to go home for the Christmas break. Kevin spent the evening before they left to go home with Terri. They celebrated the holiday and exchanged gifts.

The next morning Terri left at noon and headed for St. Louis. Kevin had an eleven o' clock class and left for Iowa after the class was over.

He stopped for lunch at the Lake of the Ozarks and afterwards he called Terri. She was just past Sullivan and on her last trek to St. Louis. They talked until she got into St. Louis county traffic and told Kevin she had better hang up and pay attention to her driving. So they told each other that they loved each other and Kevin told her to call him later.

Terri's parents were so happy to see her and had planned on taking her the "The Hill" for dinner. The Hill was a well known Italian community in St. Louis with wonderful Italian restaurants. She called Sally and she joined them. After dinner Terri and Sally took off for Ted Drew's Frozen Custard, one of their favorite places for frozen custard. Terri filled Sally in on college and her relationship with Kevin.

Sally was all ears and was very pleased how wonderful it was for Terri and Kevin to be having such a special relationship.

The girls headed back to Terri's house and Terri ran inside to call Kevin. Sally headed back to her house and they had so much fun.

Terri called Kevin immediately and he had only been home for thirty minutes. He apologized and said he was about to have dinner with his family and that Cat was so excited that he was home. He told her that he would call her later and told her that he loved her and Terri responded with, "Ditto."

After dinner and hearing all of Cat's amazing stories and finding out his dad needed him to work over Christmas, Kevin called Terri back. They talked for two hours and he told her that he wanted to come to St. Louis for New Year's Eve. She was so excited and told him that she would make plans.

When he got off the phone, he approached his parents about him going to St. Louis for New Year's. They agreed and gave him permission to do so.

Kevin worked for his dad until New Year's Eve. He and his family had a wonderful Christmas. His grandma and Aunt Helen were there from Des Moines. He told his grandma all about Terri and she seem pleased for him.

Kevin was all packed up and ready to leave early on New Years' Eve bright and early. It would take him about seven hours or so to get to St. Louis.

His mom made him a big breakfast and packed him a turkey sandwich, chips and bottled iced tea. His parents saw him off at seven and wished him a safe trip and also told him to give Terri their warmest wishes for the New Year. Then Kevin headed south for St. Louis.

CHAPTER 34

Kevin arrived in St. Louis before three and headed for Terri's house. When he got there he rang the doorbell and Terri answered it. She ran into his arms. They had both missed each other for the last two weeks.

Her parents had gone to the grocery store so they were alone for the next hour. When her parents returned Kevin greeted them and offered to help bring in the groceries. They were eating out that night but Mrs. Carter was planning on cooking on New Year's Day because a few of their friends were coming over.

Kevin asked Terri where they would be going for dinner because he really didn't have dress clothes with him. All he had was Dockers, a sweater and loafers. She told him that would be fine. Her parents were taking them to the Spaghetti Factory downtown at her request. It is very casual dress. It was one of Terri's favorite places and she loved the atmosphere and their great food.

Kevin had forgotten something in his jeep and went outside to get it. He had brought Terri and her parents six almond letter pastries from the Dutch bakery at home. Terri was thrilled. Mrs. Carter had never heard of them before so she and Terri sampled some with a cup of coffee. Mr. Carter thought they were excellent and thanked Kevin for bringing them and then she gave him a big hug. Terri looked at Kevin and gave him a big wink and Kevin smiled.

Terri told Kevin that after dinner they were going to meet up with Sally and her new boyfriend, Roger. They would meet them in Clayton at a coffee and dessert place called "Cyrinos." She and Sally planned to meet two other couples there from high school and bring in the New Year with "Cherries Jubilee."

Kevin's mom had sent Terri a little Christmas present but he decided that he would give it to her that night before they went to dinner with her parents.

Kevin wanted to know what time they were leaving for dinner because he wanted to shower and shave before they left. Terri told him they would leave around seven thirty. Her dad had made an eight o'clock reservation. By then it was five thirty so Kevin went to the guest room and laid out his clothes and went to the guest bathroom to shower. When he returned to his room there was a box of chocolates on the bed with a note from the Carters. It said, "Welcome Kevin, we are so glad you are here to celebrate New Years with us." It was signed by Terri's parents. Kevin was really touched by their thoughtfulness. He dressed and grabbed the gift for Terri from his mom and went downstairs. Terri was still in her room getting ready so Kevin sat in the family room with her dad and they visited for awhile until the two women arrived. Kevin handed Terri the gift and she opened it immediately. The card inside was from Kevin's parents and Cat. It was a beautiful music box that had been made by the Dutch with a carving of the top of the windmill in the town square of Pella. It played, "Wind Beneath My Wings."

Terri loved it and gave Kevin a big hug. She said she wanted to call them the next day to thank them.

Then they headed for dinner in two cars. The Carters were going to friends after dinner and Terri and Kevin were headed for "Cyrinos." Kevin and Terri took her car because she knew her way around St. Louis and that was easier than Kevin driving.

They arrived at The Spaghetti Factory at seven fifty. It was very crowded but since her dad had made reservations they only had to wait about twenty minutes. The four of them had a great meal and Terri smiled most of the time because she knew it was not her dad's deal for New Year's Eve. He would much rather be at some fancy steak house. After dinner, Terri hugged her parents and thanked them for a great dinner. Kevin also gave Mrs. Carter a hug and shook hands with Mr. Carter and thanked them both immensely for dinner.

Shortly they were in Terri's car and headed to Clayton. Terri had to drive around for awhile to find a parking spot. Then she found one only two blocks away.

They walked to the dessert place and Sally and Roger and one of the other couples were there. Sally had put their name in for a table of eight. She was told that it could be eleven or so before they were seated. Well it was only ten forty-five so Terri and Kevin went for a walk outside. Kevin just wanted to get his hands on her and kiss her. Pretty soon Roger came looking for them and said the table was ready. It was eleven thirty by then. They were seated and all eight decided on the "Cherries Jubilee." Terri ordered a coke, Kevin an iced tea with lemon and the others either had coffee or soft drinks.

Party hats and noise makers were the center pieces on their table. They all put the hats on and at about eleven fifty the waiter came and started the cherries. At exactly midnight the waiter flamed the dessert. The setting was perfect and all the couples kissed each other as the waiter served the warm dessert over ice cream. The place was roaring with horns and whistles and people laughing. It was a perfect night.

They got home around two fifteen and Terri's parents were in the kitchen waiting for them. Mrs. Carter told them that she had prepared two items for them to taste. They were supposed to give you good luck for the New Year. One was black-eyed peas and the other was pickled herring. Kevin told them his little sister almost threw up trying to eat it but he actually like it. Mrs. Carter smiled and served her good luck foods.

Afterwards, everyone was off to bed. Kevin walked Terri to the doorway of her room, took her in his arms, thanked her for the wonderful New Years and kissed her so passionately that she could hardly breathe. He told her he loved her and she told him that he was an amazing man and she loved him too. With that, Terri went into her room and Kevin went to the guest room. He dressed down to his boxers fell into bed and crashed. It had been a long day and he was ready for some sleep. However, he dreamed of Terri all night.

CHAPTER 35

The next morning Kevin got up, showered and shaved. He dressed casual and went downstairs where he found Mr. Carter in the kitchen preparing an enormous breakfast. He poured himself a cup of coffee and asked if he could help with breakfast but was told to enjoy his coffee and watch how to make a magnificent breakfast.

Sausage, biscuits, gravy, fruit, potatoes and scrambled eggs were on the menu. Mr. Carter always cooked this breakfast on New Year's Day and his wife and Terri loved it.

Then the ladies came down and wanted to know if breakfast was ready. Mr. Carter said to give him ten minutes because the biscuits were in the oven.

Kevin jumped up and poured Terri and her mom a cup of coffee. He figured it was a morning to take care of the women in their lives.

Terri gave him a grin and Kevin blew her a kiss.

The four of them sat down to a terrific breakfast and afterwards Mrs. Carter served a yummy dessert of bread pudding and amaretto sauce.

The ladies agreed to clean up and Kevin and Mr. Carter headed to the den to sit by the fire.

Mr. Carter was very curious about Kevin and his feelings for Terri. He asked Kevin and Kevin was honest and told Mr. Carter that he was deeply in love with his daughter.

Mr. Carter had already figured that out and just smiled.

The ladies joined them in the den and Mrs. Carter started telling them all what needed to be done before her guests arrived at four.

So then the four of them got their directions from Mrs. Carter and they all got busy.

Everything was ready to go by three so Terri and Kevin headed up to shower and dress for the party.

At three forty-five the doorbell rang and Kevin was the only one downstairs to answer the door. When he opened the door, he was so amazed that he could hardly speak. It was his mom, dad and Cat. He hugged them all and before he said a word his mom told him that Mrs. Carter had called them and invited them to the party. He could hardly believe what he was hearing.

Mrs. Carter came down and saw the Ruble family reunion. Kevin introduced her to his parents and little sister and thanked her dearly for inviting them.

Then Terri and her dad arrived and they were all in the process of getting acquainted and some of the other guests started arriving. Mrs. Carter told her husband to be the bartender and Mr. Ruble offered to help.

Sally came with her parents, her boyfriend and her younger brother who was about Cat's age. Cat and Marty really hit it off and spent their time having fun together.

There were about thirty or forty people at the party. It was a cocktail and appetizer party and everyone who attended seemed to have a good time.

Afterwards, Mrs. Ruble helped clean up while others sat in the den and visited. The Ruble's had a reservation at a nearby hotel and they were ready to go there. Kevin and Terri thanked them for coming and they left for the hotel around eleven. Kevin told his folks he would see them in the morning. Mr. Carter suggested they all meet for breakfast at ten at the hotel restaurant and everyone agreed. They all hugged and the Ruble's were off to the hotel.

Kevin woke early, showered, shaved and dressed. He stopped by Terri's room and she was also dressed and ready to go. He took her in his arms and kissed her and told her that both their parents had really surprised him.

They went downstairs and joined Mr. Carter in the kitchen for a cup of coffee. Mrs. Carter joined them in about fifteen minutes and soon they were off to the hotel to meet the Ruble's for breakfast.

CHAPTER 36

They all enjoyed visiting at breakfast. Mr. Carter excused himself from the table and secretly went to pay the bill. When they were ready to leave Mr. Ruble asked for the check and was told that it was taken care of. Mr. Ruble really wanted to repay the Carter's for all they had done but it was too late.

They all left the restaurant and they all said their goodbyes in the hotel lobby. The Ruble's thanked them and headed up to pack and head back to Iowa. Before they parted the Ruble's invited the Carter's to Pella for the tulip festival in the spring. The Carter's told them that they would let them know later.

All the farewells were made and Kevin, Terri and the Carter's headed home so the kids could pack up and head for Springfield.

The Rubles packed up and headed for Iowa by noon. Kevin and Terri were on their way by three.

It was an easy drive to Springfield. Kevin in his jeep followed Terri in her car. He went to Drury to help her unload and move into her dorm. It was a rather warm day and Kevin asked her to go get something to eat with him. They headed out to a pizza place that was very popular with the college crowd. Afterwards he took Terri back to her dorm. They hugged and kissed for about fifteen minutes and Kevin told her goodnight and that he loved her.

He then went to his dorm and started unloading his jeep and hauling his luggage into the dorm.

His roommate Jake was already there. They visited for a bit and then Kevin started preparing for his classes the next day.

He called Terri before bed to tell her what a great weekend he had and how he appreciated his parents' invitation to the party.

They talked about fifteen minutes and told each other how much they loved each other and then said goodnight to each other.

Then all of Kevin's suite mates were there. He visited with Frank and the others before retiring to bed. He set his alarm for seven in the morning so he would have time to shower, shave and have breakfast before his nine o' clock class. He also called Terri to tell her good morning and they chatted for a few minutes. Terri had to be in class at nine also.

They both knew that their education came before their relationship and knew that the time they spent together would be limited. They planned to see each other on weekends and talk on the phone every day.

Kevin had a really hard eighteen hour semester with his math classes. His advanced math instructor told him that he would be giving some hard challenges throughout the semester.

Terri was interested in elementary education and decided that would be her major and she would become a teacher.

They both were studying a great deal and doing really well on exams. Their social life wasn't exactly fulfilling but they managed it.

Kevin was trying hard not to spend too much of his savings so a lot of their dates were just spending time together or eating at McDonalds.

Spring break was approaching but it was not yet time for the tulip festival in Pella. They decided that they would both go to their own homes for the break and spend time with their families.

Cat was especially excited that her big brother would be home for one whole week. Mr. Ruble had some work that he needed Kevin's help with. Kevin also helped his dad order supplies because with his math skills he could figure up how many supplies to order, including nails and roof shingles.

The week went by quickly and Kevin was on his way back to school. He told his parents that he and Terri would try to be home for the tulip festival in six weeks. It would be a quick weekend trip.

The Rubles had heard from the Carters and it was sounding like they would be there too if the kids were coming.

With a lack of hotels and motels in Pella, Mrs. Ruble was planning on everyone staying at her house.

CHAPTER 37

Kevin went straight to Drury when he got back to Springfield. He knew that Terri was already there because they had been on their phones several times that day.

They were so happy to see each other that they could hardly keep their hands off of each other.

Kevin's dad had paid him three hundred for his help while he was home. Kevin decided to take Terri out for a steak dinner.

They really enjoyed each other's company through dinner and both thought the dinner was superb. They were having dessert and Kevin told Terri that he thought it was time for them to take another step in their relationship. Terri did not look surprised but instead agreed with him one hundred percent.

They left the restaurant and went to a hotel and checked in. It was rather awkward for both of them so they decided to take a whirlpool together. As Kevin undressed Terri, he was trembling and so was she. It was the first time they had seen each other naked. Both jumped into the whirlpool and started playing around. They were kissing and hugging and exploring each other's bodies. Then they hopped out of the tub, dried each other and headed for the bed. Luckily, Kevin had brought a condom for the occasion. They cuddled, hugged, kissed and giggled. Kevin knew it was time so he put on the condom and lay on top of Terri. As she opened her legs, he entered her very easily. She groaned but pulled him closer inside of her.

They made love for two hours and professed their love for each other. It was truly a magnificent experience for both of them.

They both jumped in the shower together to rinse off and decided they had better get back to their dorms to get ready for classes the next day.

When Kevin dropped Terri off at her dorm and walked her to her room, he held her tightly at her door, kissed her passionately and told her he loved her more than ever. She repeated what he had said and thanked him for being so sincere and gentle for her first time.

He smiled, kissed her again and said goodnight and that he would call her in the morning before classes.

He could hardly sleep that night because all he could think about was how wonderful it was having sex with Terri.

Terri didn't sleep a wink all night. All she thought about was Kevin and what a wonderful man he was. She had no regrets whatsoever of having sex with him. In her mind, life was good.

The next day it was back to classes. She called Kevin and thanked him for a wonderful evening. He told her that when he got back to the dorm that he was in a daze and accomplished nothing. They both told each other how much they loved each other and it was off to class for both of them.

CHAPTER 38

Six weeks had passed and it was the time to head to Pella for the tulip festival. Terri's parents were leaving the same day. All would be staying at the Ruble's. Terri would bunk with Cat. The Carter's would have Kevin's room and he would be sleeping in the basement in a makeshift bedroom.

Everyone arrived at about the same time. Mrs. Carter was totally amazed how all the sidewalks in town were lined with blooming tulips. Mrs. Ruble had prepared a pot roast for dinner and they all enjoyed the beginning of a festival weekend.

The next day Mrs. Ruble had to open her store and Cat went with her to help. Mr. Ruble showed the rest around town and they ended up at the Dutch bakery for an almond letter.

The Carter's were very impressed with all the Dutch architecture in the town and especially the huge windmill in the town square. They went to Mrs. Ruble's shop and loved it. Mrs. Carter bought about three hundred dollars worth of merchandise. It was for her and some were gifts for friends.

Saturday afternoon they went to the tulip parade and then enjoyed the entertainment on the grandstand at the town square under the windmill.

Starting at five all sorts of food booths opened up and both families had dinner at a large picnic table outside. Luckily it was about sixty degrees. Everyone got different foods from the booths and then they all shared their discoveries of the local cuisine.

It was about eight and they all headed back to the Ruble's. The men had a sniffle of brandy and the ladies a glass of wine. Kevin, Terri and Cat headed for the basement to play ping pong. At the end of the tournament, Cat was the winner and jumping for joy.

Sunday morning they all went to breakfast at a local café. Then they went to the bakery and the Carter's bought almond letters and Dutch apple bread to take home.

It was time for the Carter's to get going and they thanked the Ruble's for their hospitality. They loaded up all their goodies, hugged and kissed everyone and headed for St. Louis.

Kevin and Terri packed up his jeep and were ready to leave. His dad asked Kevin to join him in the garage for a moment. When they were by themselves, Mr. Ruble asked Kevin how it was going with Terri. He told his dad that their relationship was better than ever.

Then his dad asked him if he had made love to her yet. Kevin was floored and started turning red. He then decided to tell the truth because he and his dad always were truthful with each other. He told his dad that they had made love one time and how wonderful it was. His dad warned him to be very careful and that a pregnancy was not in his near future. He explained that he used a condom and everything was okay. His dad told him to be very careful and the two of them hugged each other. They had a great deal of respect for each other and Mr. Ruble trusted his son.

Kevin and Terri hugged and kissed everyone before jumping in the jeep to head for Springfield. First, Kevin wanted to go by his friends' house to say hi and see how they were doing. They were there about twenty minutes so it was about one or so before they got on their way.

Terri's mom called twice during their trip and told Terri to be sure and call her when she got back to school.

They only stopped once for gas and a restroom break. They went through McDonald's drive-thru for something to eat and ate while traveling. So they made good time and pulled into Terri's dorm by ten. Kevin carried her things to her room for her and they said goodnight with a hug and kiss. Kevin then headed to his dorm across town.

He parked the jeep, grabbed his duffle bag and the bag of goodies his mom had sent and headed for his room. Jake was asleep so Kevin tried to be quiet. He called his parents to let them know that he and Terri had made it back safely. Then he hopped into bed because he was exhausted.

His alarm went off at five in the morning and he got up to finish a couple of assignments before class at nine.

Then he showered, dressed and called Terri around eight. She was up and ready for class. After a short talk, Kevin headed to the cafeteria for breakfast and then off to his first class.

CHAPTER 39

The rest of the semester flew by and Kevin and Terri only saw each other on weekends but they talked at least twice each day.

They were both studying for finals and finishing up papers they had to turn in.

Kevin made all A's in his math classes. He ended the semester with a 3.8 grade point average because he got a B in a fine arts class that he had to take for his basic requirements.

Terri ended up with a 4.0. she was so thrilled and Kevin was so proud of her. They spent the weekend together at a hotel before heading home for the summer. They made love several times but when Monday morning came they were forced into saying goodbye and heading for home. They did not make any plans when they would get together over the summer but they both knew that somehow they would.

They talked several time to each other while traveling. Terri was home in four hours and Kevin was still on the road with more than four hours to go. When he stopped for gas, he went for a jog around the gas station to refresh himself and gear up for the rest of his trip. He grabbed a sandwich and iced tea at the station and was back on the road headed home. He was in Iowa soon and he knew that he didn't have far to go.

When he pulled into the driveway, Cat came running out to meet him. His mom saved him some dinner and after eating and visiting they all went to bed.

Kevin's dad knew that Kevin was tired from the trip so they let him sleep in. He told Cat to tell Kevin that he didn't have to come to work that day. So when he woke up and went to the kitchen, Cat told him that their dad said he did not have to work that day. So after eating, Kevin showered and shaved and he and Cat headed to town to his mom's store. Kevin helped her unpack some merchandise and Cat headed down the street to hopefully find one of her friends.

Kevin seemed a little down to his mom so she asked him why he was so down. He told her that he was very glad to be home but that he really missed Terri and didn't know when he would see her over the summer. His mom suggested inviting her for the fourth of July. Kevin told her that after the ordeal at Chicago last year that she probably wouldn't want to fly.

Mrs. Ruble felt his feelings and suggested that he fly to St. Louis for the fourth. She knew that St. Louis had an extraordinary celebration at the St. Louis arch on the fourth. Kevin smiled and told his mom that she was the best mom ever.

That night she told her husband her idea and he agreed and got on the computer to make Kevin an airline reservation. When they told Kevin at breakfast the next day, he was so excited and hugged and kissed both his parents and then went to call Terri.

She was so happy that Kevin would be coming for the fourth. He told her that he loved her and would let her know when his flight would arrive.

Then he hurried out of the house with his dad to get to work on a new library that his dad was building for the city of Pella.

Kevin worked ten hour days to help out his dad with the construction. He was hoping that they would complete the library before he went back to school in the fall. His dad was hoping for the same.

CHAPTER 40

It was Thursday before the fourth and Kevin headed to Des Moines to catch his plane for St. Louis. Everything was on time and in a couple of hours he landed in St. Louis.

Terri and her dad were there to meet him. He ran toward Terri and lifter her off her feet, spinning around and kissing her passionately. Her dad just stood and watched and smiled. Then Kevin gave Mr. Carter a huge hug and told him that he was so glad to be there.

They headed home to get Mrs. Carter to go to a restaurant on The Hill. They all enjoyed Italian food and then Terri told her folks that she wanted to go home and spend some alone time with Kevin.

When they got there she took Kevin aside and they headed for the patio. There they hugged and kissed and were nearly ready for sex but both of them knew that they couldn't do it there.

Terri told Kevin that maybe later in her bedroom would be more appropriate. Then they went inside and spent the evening with her parents watching TV and visiting.

Kevin excused himself and went to the guest room where he was staying to call his parents. They were pleased that he had arrived safely and was having a good time. Cat told him to tell Terri that she really missed her.

When Kevin came back downstairs, the Carters were heading to bed and told him goodnight and they would prepare breakfast before they all headed out to the St. Louis arch for the fourth of July fair.

He thanked them for their hospitality and Mrs. Carter gave him a hug. Terri gave both her parents a hug and thanked them for letting Kevin visit.

After her parents went to bed, Terri told Kevin that she wanted to go upstairs to her room. When they got to Terri's room, Kevin told her goodnight and that as much as he wanted to make love to her that he didn't feel right about it. He had a great deal of respect for her parents and their home. Terri was somewhat disappointed but she understood. Kevin was always such a gentleman and mannerly about everything.

So they kissed and hugged goodnight and Kevin went to his room. He could hardly go to sleep because he knew that he could have easily been making love to Terri. He set his phone alarm for seven and eventually went to sleep.

When the alarm went off, he jumped up and headed to the shower. Then he shaved and blew his hair dry and also added a bit of Terri's favorite cologne to his neck. Then he decided he would wear shorts and a Missouri State t-shirt. He then went downstairs and Mr. Carter was in the kitchen frying bacon and making waffles. After their greeting, Kevin helped himself to a cup of coffee. About that time Terri and her mom showed up. Terri was wearing shorts, a Drury t-shirt and sandals. He thought she looked gorgeous and gave her a kiss.

They all sat at the kitchen table and enjoyed their breakfast. Mr. Carter announced that they had better get going because the parade started at ten. So they all piled into Mr. Carter's SUV and headed for the parade.

When the parade ended, they went to a tavern in Soulard for lunch. Kevin always offered to pay but Mr. Carter told him that was not necessary. After lunch, Mr. and Mrs. Carter were ready to head home.

Kevin and Terri sat on the patio for awhile and then Terri told Kevin that she wanted to head for the arch to watch some of the concerts. Sally and her new boyfriend were going to meet them there.

There was lots of entertainment throughout the rest of the afternoon and at seven a big name singer was to perform. Terri and Sally were anxious to see "Brooks and Dunn" on stage. The four of them grabbed a burger and coke at a booth and headed to the main stage.

Sure enough the concert was a huge success. Kevin could not believe the thousands of people there. It was quite different from the Fourth of July celebration in Pella.

When the concert ended the two couples said farewell and Kevin and Terri headed out to find Terri's car. It took about thirty minutes to get to her car and another hour to get back to her parents because of heavy traffic. Kevin was glad that Terri was driving.

They greeted her parents and talked about how good the concert was. Terri then took Kevin to the patio so that she could be alone with him. Her parents said goodnight and went on to bed.

Terri talked Kevin into making love to her on the patio. He told her he needed to go upstairs to get a condom. She told him that wasn't necessary because she had been on the pill since the beginning of the summer. Kevin chose to be double safe and went to get a condom anyway.

When Kevin took his clothes off, Terri chuckled at him and told him that his butt was white as snow compared to the rest of him. Then he came back with a comment how white her butt was and also her breast.

They started making out and in a few minutes Kevin was entering her with his usual gentleness. They seemed to be a good fit and satisfied each other shortly. Then he held her in his arms so tight and told her how much he loved her.

After another thirty minutes naked on the patio they both decided that they should go inside and head for bed.

It had been one super day and evening for both of them.

CHAPTER 41

The next day was the fourth. Kevin and Terri slept in until about ten. Kevin was surprised when he woke up and saw what time it was. He jumped up and went to Terri's room. She had finished getting dressed. He kissed her and thanked her again for the wonderful evening they had together. She told him to get busy and jump in the shower.

Kevin took a quick shower, shaved and got ready for the day. He put on shorts and a red and blue polo shirt and was ready in twenty minutes. When he went downstairs, the Carters were reading the paper and Mrs. Carter told him there was coffee in the kitchen.

Terri warmed up some egg casserole for both of them and afterwards they both cleaned up the kitchen. Kevin was having a hard time keeping his hands off Terri.

The day would be uneventful until about six that evening when they all would head for the arch and the fireworks. Kevin and Terri went for a drive and she took him by the St. Louis zoo and then to the planetarium to watch a science movie. He really enjoyed it and sincerely thanked her.

They went back to Terri's house, had a snack and before long the four of them were headed for the arch. Mr. Carter had a parking pass in a garage close so they didn't have to walk far.

The concert was unreal with "Earth, Wind and Fire" and a special appearance by Stevie Wonder. Kevin could not believe how great it was and what a wonderful time he was having.

Then at nine thirty everyone gathered to watch the fireworks on the riverfront. Kevin kept taking pictures on his cell because he had never seen such spectacular fireworks.

They all arrived home around one in the morning. All were tired and headed for bed.

Sunday morning came too early for Kevin and Terri. He had a one o' clock flight for Des Moines.

Mrs. Carter made a huge breakfast and they all enjoyed it and each other's company. Kevin kept thanking the Carters for having him and what a wonderful time he was having.

At ten, Kevin and Terri headed for the airport. They were both sad but they had had a spectacular weekend.

When they arrived, Kevin kept his duffle bag with him because it would be okay for a carry-on.

They could hardly pull each other apart when it came time for Kevin to get on the plane. They hugged and kissed and finally they heard a last call to board the plane. Kevin gave her one last loving kiss and took off running to catch his plane.

On the flight all he could think about was Terri and wished that they were married and never had to be apart.

When he arrived in Des Moines he retrieved his jeep in the parking garage and headed for Pella.

On the way he called Terri and told her that he already missed her. It was about an hour drive and they talked the whole time. He told her that he would call her again later that night.

When he arrived home, as usual, Cat came running out of the house to greet him. He really loved his little sister and she loved him back even more.

His parents were out back on the patio. Mr. Ruble had just finished mowing the lawn and Mrs. Ruble had been trimming bushes and flowers. They were glad to see that Kevin was home safe and both hugged him generously. Kevin really loved his parents and always did his best for them.

Kevin went to the kitchen for a snack. His mom told him not to eat too much because they were having steaks for dinner. Kevin knew that he would be the one grilling the steaks because that was his job when he was home. So he snacked on some veggies and dip and had a glass of milk.

He took his duffle bag upstairs and unpacked. Almost everything was dirty and needed to go to the laundry room. He started loading his clothes and his mom stopped him and told him to go visit with his dad on the patio and she would do his laundry. He thanked her with a hug and headed outside to the patio.

He and his dad discussed business and what needed to be done on the construction sites where they were building two homes. One was for a client and the other was a spec home that his dad decided to invest in.

His dad asked him about his trip to St. Louis and Kevin gave him all the details and what a great trip he had. Mr. Ruble was glad for him. He did tell him that he was missed at the Fourth of July dance and his old partner Jennifer wanted to know where he was. Kevin grinned at that and told his dad that he could have filled in for him. Mr. Ruble told Kevin that he did just that and it was really fun. Kevin wished that he could have seen that.

Mr. Ruble went to get a beer and brought Kevin one. He told Kevin they had better get the grill going for the steaks. They visited some more and sipped on their beer. His dad went for a second but Kevin declined. He still had half of his left

Kevin's mom came out with four beautiful sirloins all marinated and told the guys that Cat was making a salad and the twice baked potatoes and bread were in the oven keeping warm. Kevin decided to get the steaks on the grill. His mom returned with a glass of wine and an iced tea with lemon for Kevin to supervise his cooking the steaks. The whole family liked them medium so Kevin knew it would only take fifteen minutes or less.

The four of them all ate on the patio that evening and everyone raved to Cat how delicious her salad was. She had added some walnuts and feta cheese with a vinaigrette dressing.

All said the steaks were perfectly cooked and they had a terrific time having dinner together. After dinner Mr. Ruble said that he would clean up and do the dishes since he hadn't helped with the cooking.

Kevin went to his room to call Terri. She answered on the first ring and they talked for an hour. He filled her in on what was going on at his house and she did the same. She and her parents had also had steaks and ate on the patio.

They told each other how much they loved each other and how much they missed one another. After hanging up, Kevin went downstairs to tell everyone goodnight and that he was headed for bed. He told his dad that he would be up early and ready to go to work with him in the morning.

CHAPTER 42

The morning came and Kevin and his dad were up at five to have a bite of breakfast and be on the job by six. Mr. Ruble told Kevin that he had put the spec home on hold. He was taking one of the employees with him to work on the library building. Kevin was to take the other two workers to work on the house for a client. They both left the house by quarter till six to meet with the employees and give them their assignments for the week.

Kevin's dad pulled him off his job a couple of times to help at the library. The old library was a small one room brick building. The new one was going to have a lobby and four large rooms and two lofts. Kevin was helping to put up the dry wall since all the framing was done. The windows were in and it was under roof.

When Kevin went back to the house the two workers were moving right along framing it up. Kevin had designed all the basics and he was pleased how well everything was coming together.

Mr. Ruble had furnished lots of bottled water for the workers and told them all that they had to take a lunch break. They had been working in ninety degree weather and he didn't want any of them to get over heated.

Kevin called Terri on every lunch break and every night. On Sundays they would talk for hours. Kevin even went with Cat to the lake for a swim sometimes. Cat really had fun wrestling with her brother in the water and having races.

Sunday night was usually a cook out at the Rubles but they ate inside in the air conditioned house because it was so hot outside.

The library was ready to be painted so Mr. Ruble hired a painter in town to do it. That way he and the workers helping him could help Kevin and his crew on the house. The painter was excellent and had the whole place painted in two weeks. Mr. Ruble and Kevin went to install al the shelves that they had already built and stained.

In two more weeks the library was finished and the town board was extremely pleased with the results. They immediately paid Mr. Ruble what they owed him and volunteers started helping move from the old to the new. It was a beautiful library and the Ruble's were very proud to be a part of it. Cat was even one of the volunteers helping with the move.

CHAPTER 43

Summer was about to come to an end. Kevin would be a junior and Terri a sophomore. Kevin and Jake decided to stay in Blair-Shannon in the same room. Frank and his roommates were too but the other two guys had left school. So there would be two new guys to get used to.

He left for school on September first and so did Terri. Their classes would start the day after Labor Day which was the third.

Terri was waiting for him when he arrived. They went to get a bite to eat and then he took her to Lake Springfield for a walk before dark.

Kevin had bought Terri a promise ring and wanted to give it to her. He told her that he promised to love and cherish her forever and that he knew he really wanted to be married to her.

With tears in her eyes, Terri accepted the ring and they headed for the hotel to spend the night. Their love making was extra special that night and for the first time, Kevin did not use a condom and the sensations he felt were amazing.

They held each other and fell asleep naked and in each other's arms. When Kevin woke up Terri was in the shower so he went and joined her. He told her that this was how every morning would be when they were married.

They checked out by noon and went to lunch. Terri bought since Kevin had paid for the hotel. She told Kevin that she had applied for a small job at Drury and would only be working two hours a day and it would help her to have some spending money.

Kevin had no problem with that because she always carried a straight A grade point average.

He took her back to her dorm, kissed her goodbye and headed for his dorm to move in. As usual, Jake was already there and starting to unpack.

Frank and his roommate showed up and then the two new guys, Dave and Ron. They all got acquainted and seemed to hit it off. Dave was a business major and Ron's was chemistry. All six of them seemed to be focused on school, except Jake, and Kevin knew that he would have to keep him motivated.

Terri had a new roommate this year and she was a junior and her name was Barb. Barb was from St. Louis and she and Terri really hit it off. They were both education majors and somewhat on the quiet side. It was a perfect match for roommates.

Classes started and Kevin's math professor told him that he would qualify to start on his master's his senior year as long as his grades were good. Kevin was thrilled to hear that and promised that he would.

It was a hard semester because he was taking eighteen hours but so was Terri. If she went to summer school two times she could graduate in three years.

It was a very hard semester for both of them. When Thanksgiving came, Kevin went home with Terri. His folks were a little disappointed and poor Cat cold hardly stand the thought of it. But her grandma and aunt would be there. She also had a new boyfriend named Ken. He was a year older but they were having a great deal of fun together.

Kevin had a great time in St. Louis with the Carter's for Thanksgiving. He called his folks and talked to everyone. Cat told him all about Ken. Kevin was quite amused hearing all of Cat's tales.

It came time on Sunday for Terri and Kevin to head for Springfield. Kevin told her that Missouri State held a huge Christmas dance and wanted her to go with him. She immediately said yes and asked if it was formal. He told her no, it was just dressy.

They both got back into studying. Terri had two papers due and Kevin was going up for his master's exam to see if he would qualify early so that he could start the program the next semester.

He did very well on the exam and was accepted one semester early. He called his parents and they were so very proud of his accomplishments.

It was a few days before the Christmas dance and Kevin's new roommate, Dave, needed a date. Kevin asked Terri to see if Barb would be willing to go with Dave.

Barb told Terri that she sure would so a double date was set. Kevin and Dave even bought corsages for the girls and arrived just on time to pick them up at their dorm.

After introductions, Dave almost swept Barb off her feet with his appeal. Kevin and Terri smiled at how they seemed to have hit it off.

They went to the dance and had a fabulous time dancing and talking. When it was time to take the girls home Dave was disappointed because he wanted to spend more time with Barb. So they exchanged phone numbers and to Barb's surprise, Dave kissed her goodnight.

On the way back to their dorm Dave kept thanking Kevin for fixing him up with Barb.

The next morning both Kevin and Dave were calling the girls to let them know what a great evening it was.

Three days later, it was time for both Terri and Kevin to head home for Christmas break. They stood holding on to each other for thirty minutes before Terri got in her car and drove off. Kevin got in his jeep and headed for Iowa. They talked several times while driving. When Kevin got to the Iowa border it had started to snow. He already knew that Terri had made it home safely. The snow kept coming down and by the time he was an hour from Pella the roads were getting pretty bad. So he put the jeep in four wheel drive and drove very slow. The last hour of the drive took over two hours because of the conditions.

He arrived safely at home and his parents and Cat were very happy to see him. Then he called Terri to let her know that he was home. They kissed over the phone and then Kevin went to the kitchen and announced that he was hungry.

His mom was preparing dinner. It was a chicken casserole and was already done but was in the oven to stay warm. Cat set the table and the four of them sat down for a yummy dinner. Mrs. Ruble had also made homemade biscuits to go with the casserole.

After dinner Cat and her dad cleaned up and Kevin and his mom went to sit by the fire in the den. The snow was still coming down. It sure was looking like it was going to be a white Christmas in Pella.

The next morning Kevin got his dad's snow blower out and started clearing the driveway and sidewalks. Cat came out with the snow shovel and began to help. There was probably six to eight inches but it was a dry snow so the snow blower did a pretty good job.

That afternoon after lunch they put up the family Christmas tree and started decorating it. There were several ornaments that Kevin and Cat had made when they were young and they both got a big kick out of looking at them. His mom told Kevin to put all of them on the tree.

It was two days until Christmas. Kevin's grandma and aunt were going to drive from Des Moines the next day. Mr. Ruble called the highway department and found out that the interstate was all clear and safe for travel.

His grandma and aunt arrived the next day safely. Grandma stayed in Kevin's room and his aunt bunked in with Cat. Kevin moved to the basement in their makeshift bedroom.

He took pictures of the snow and their Christmas tree and sent them to Terri on his phone. She responded shortly with pictures of their tree but said that there was no snow in St. Louis.

Later Kevin called her and they talked for an hour and professed their love for each other. Kevin's grandma overheard some of their conversation and she knew that this was probably the real thing. She asked Kevin about him and Terri's relationship and got all good responses from Kevin.

Grandma seemed very pleased and happy for Kevin. He was twenty years old and absolutely knew what he wanted out of life. The number one on his list was Terri.

He sent her a dozen roses for Christmas and she was thrilled. She called him to thank him when she received them on Christmas Eve morning. They talked for two hours and laughed and cried because they missed each other so much.

Christmas morning came and when all the family got up, they went to the living room. There were gifts everywhere. The biggest and most surprising gift was from grandma. She gave Kevin and Cat five hundred dollars and they could hardly believe it. It was a wonderful Christmas and after dinner and everything else, Kevin went to call Terri. She had a good Christmas too and they talked for an hour.

It was getting very late so Kevin said his goodnights to all the family and gave his grandma a big kiss and thanked her for her generous gift.

Kevin slept for ten hours that night and when he finally got up, it was snowing again. All the snow and cold weather was really hurting his dad's construction business. However, his dad had saved a great deal of money for the cold weather months.

So after breakfast he went to clear the driveway and clean the snow off of everyone's cars. By noon or so, the sun came out and his aunt and grandma wanted to head home. Mr. Ruble called the highway department and the interstate was clear all the way to Des Moines. They left about three and called at five and said they made it home and had no problems. Their neighbor had even cleared their driveway.

Mrs. Ruble was very relieved to hear that they were home safe.

Kevin called Terri that night and told her about all the snow. He told her that he and Cat were going snowboarding the next day. Terri told him to be careful and that she really missed him. He doubted that he would see her until they got back to school after the first of the year.

The next morning he and Cat grabbed their snowboards out of the garage and headed to the best spot to snowboard. Iowa was mostly flat country but there were some good hills near Pella where they could go.

They had such a terrific time all morning and Cat thanked him over and over for taking her.

It warmed up the next day and some of the snow was melting. It was three days until New Year's and he wanted to go to St. Louis to be with Terri. He realized that it would not happen because now St. Louis was having snow and ice.

In a couple of days was New Year's Eve. Kevin and his family had prime rib and his mom's famous twice baked potatoes. She also made homemade yeast rolls and Cat made the salad. They all celebrated New Years after dinner and then Kevin went to call Terri. He told her Happy New Year and that weather permitting that he would see her in Springfield in a few days.

The next day it started warming up in Pella and also in St. Louis. On January third Kevin packed the jeep and headed for Springfield by eight in the morning. Terri left St. Louis at about eleven. All the roads were clear of snow. They talked on the phone several times during their drive.

When he got to Springfield, he went to Drury and Terri was waiting for him at her dorm. They hugged and kissed in the lobby for about an hour. Then they went to dinner together. Kevin took her back to her dorm and told her goodnight and that he loved her with all of his heart.

He then went to his dorm and unloaded the jeep and went to his room. As usual Jake was already there so they caught each other up about their holiday.

Classes started the next day. Kevin was prepared and went to class at nine after calling Terri. She too was about to head for class.

Here he was a junior and she a sophomore and time seemed to be passing quickly. They got together on weekends and due to Kevin's grandma's Christmas gift, he could afford a motel for them so they could be together to make love to each other.

The semester flew by and now it was time for spring break. They wanted to spend it together but could not figure out how they could.

Kevin told Terri that if they were married that it wouldn't be a problem. So they spent a couple of days at the hotel and both headed home for the rest of spring break.

Kevin worked for his dad and helped paint the spec home and Mr. Ruble had already had a couple interested in buying it. His dad always paid him well and when the break was over, he headed back to Springfield.

The two of them were so busy with their studies that they only saw each other about once a week. Both Terri and Kevin finished the year with a 4.0 grade point average.

CHAPTER 44

Kevin told Jake that he was going to start looking for an apartment for him and Terri for the next year. Jake seemed okay with the idea.

Kevin searched and found a cute one bedroom on the second floor of an older couple's house on Walnut Street. He put a down payment on it for September. He then told Terri that he had rented it and wanted her to live there with him. She was so excited and told him that she had better talk this over with her parents. Kevin told her he was going to tell his parents when he got home.

He took her to the apartment and she loved it. It was totally furnished and a nice bedroom, bath, kitchen and fairly large living room. It also had a double carport for both their cars.

He told Terri to do whatever she could to convince her parents and that he would do the same.

Terri didn't think that her parents would go for it but to her surprise they said it would be alright. Mr. Carter told Terri that they would pay one half of the rent.

Kevin called his dad to see what he thought. Mr. Ruble wanted to talk it over with his wife but told Kevin it would probably be a go. When his dad called back, he gave Kevin the okay and Kevin called Terri to tell her the good news.

They both went to the apartment and signed a one semester lease.

Jake was upset because he was going to lose his roommate. He, Frank and Frank's roommate found a two bedroom apartment at "Fountain Plaza" apartments and decided to move in as soon as the semester was over.

All of them moved to their new homes and were very happy, especially Kevin and Terri. They decided that their apartment needed a little painting so Kevin told his new landlords that if they would pay for the paint that he would do all the painting himself.

So he and Terri went to the paint store and Kevin told Terri to pick out all the colors.

They returned to the apartment and Kevin started painting and Terri went shopping for a few things they would need like towels, sheets, kitchen stuff and accessories for the apartment.

They were so excited about their new place and they both spent the night there. The next day they moved from their dorms and moved everything into the apartment.

There were only two closets, one in the bedroom and one in the living room. Kevin told Terri to use the one in the bedroom and that he would make due with the smaller one in the living room.

In two days they were all set up in their new place. Kevin needed to head home to Pella so he could make some money working for his dad. Terri was staying in Springfield to go to summer school and would probably graduate early. Kevin was so proud of her.

He left for Iowa and it was a sad day for both of them. He told her that he would be back on the Fourth of July weekend.

They kissed and hugged forever before he left. Terri settled in and her mom and aunt were coming for the weekend before her classes started on Monday to check out the apartment.

Her mom and aunt loved it and took Terri shopping to stock her up on groceries and other items to dress up the apartment. Terri was pleased that they had done that for her and thanked them over and over. Then the three of them went to the mall and Mrs. Carter bought Terri some new outfits for summer school. When Sunday came, her mom and aunt took off for St. Louis. Terri had a fully stocked refrigerator and pantry so she fixed a light dinner for herself.

Then she called Kevin to tell him what a great weekend she had with her mom and aunt. He was pleased to hear it and wished her well on her first day of classes the next day.

He went to work for his dad to make some money. The spec home was done and it sold in three days. Mr. Ruble had a contract to build three pole barns for farmers and he sent Kevin out to figure out the details to build them.

Ruble Construction had all three done in two months.

Kevin was planning to go to Springfield for the Fourth of July but Terri told him that she was going to St. Louis.

Kevin decided to stay home and went to Pella's Fourth of July festivities. At the windmill, his dance partner Jennifer showed up and they put on a show for the audience.

Then, his parents and Cat headed to the high school for the fireworks display at the football field. They all had a great time and Kevin saw a lot of old friends there.

When he got home he called Terri and she too had a great fourth with her parents and they had been to the arch to watch the fireworks. He told her how much he loved her and that he missed her so much. They professed their love for each other and with kisses over the phone ended their call.

CHAPTER 45

It was a good summer for Ruble Construction and also for Mrs. Ruble's shop. Mr. Ruble had contracted to build four pole barns and had started a new home in the countryside for a client. He had to hire two more employees to keep up with the demand.

He put Kevin to work figuring up what and how much supplies they needed. It only took Kevin two days and everything they needed to get started was on order, including the bulldozer to set the formations for some of the foundations.

The house would be a very huge project and Mr. Ruble told the client that it might take a year to complete. The client was okay with that because he had another year and a half before he would retire and be ready to move in.

Kevin could hardly believe how prosperous his dad's business was considering it was in a small town in Iowa. He worked seven days a week until it was time for him to go back to school. His dad paid him well and he had about five thousand dollars saved up.

He couldn't wait to get back to Springfield and move into the apartment. Then they could start their new life together.

Terri had turned twenty in August and he would soon be twenty one. They were so much in love and the new apartment was great for them.

Terri would probably graduate at the end of the semester and she wanted to transfer to Missouri State to work on her master's degree.

Kevin had enrolled in twenty hours and was hoping to graduate in December also and then start a full time masters program in Mechanical engineering.

They loved living together and took turns cooking and doing the shopping. They hardly ever ate out because they wanted to save up their money. It was all working for them and they were pleased.

Terri's mom called her every other night to see how the new arrangement was working out. Kevin talked to his parents on weekends. They were both doing really well with their classes and both sets of parents were pleased that it was all working out.

Sally and her boyfriend Roger came to Springfield for homecoming weekend. They stayed at the apartment on a pull out bed in their old couch. The four of them had a great time. Roger took them all to dinner on Saturday night and paid the bill as a thank you for having him and Sally visit. They left at about noon on Sunday and both Terri and Kevin hit the books to study the rest of the afternoon and into the evening. They had a light late super at nine and then headed for bed to get some sleep.

Thanksgiving was coming up so they decided that they would both go home to their own parents' for the four day holiday. They both left after classes on Wednesday. Terri was home by six that evening but Kevin didn't get home until eleven. As usual, Cat was the first to greet him with hugs and kisses.

The next day was traditional Thanksgiving dinner for both families.

Kevin left by ten on Sunday morning and got to Springfield before Terri. She arrived thirty minutes later and they fell into bed to make love. They both felt like they had been apart for four months instead of four days.

The next morning it was back to the grind of classes and studying. They would both graduate in December. Kevin's graduation would be on a Friday and Terri's on a Sunday of the same weekend. Both families were coming and had reservations at the "Lamplight Inn".

It was a really great time and both parents treated them to two really nice dinners at nice restaurants while they were there.

Terri was planning to go home with Kevin for Christmas but she felt bad so she ended up going to St. Louis and Kevin to Pella. However, Kevin went to St. Louis for New Year's and all was well with both families.

When they returned to Springfield they both started their master's programs at Missouri State. They both had gotten scholarships to help pay for the tuition.

Time flew by and before long they had completed the semester and decided to stay in Springfield and go to summer school. Both of them were taking twelve hours which was a lot for summer school but they each knew they could handle it.

After summer school they both only had one semester left to complete their masters degree. They neither one had to take a heavy load to finish their program.

Kevin was approached by a company in Kansas City and they wanted him to come for an interview. He and Terri drove up there one Sunday for his interview on Monday morning.

He was offered a job for a great deal of money and accepted it. Terri was so thrilled so she started applying for teaching jobs in the Kansas City area.

Within one month she had accepted a job in a Lee Summit elementary school and would be teaching fourth grade.

She was thrilled and Kevin was so pleased with her. They soon started looking for an apartment and with help from Kevin's company they found and rented a two bedroom apartment with two bathrooms in Lee Summit. Terri could even walk to work if she wanted.

So after graduating with their masters degrees they loaded up and headed to Kansas City. Kevin had been given an advance so when they got there and unloaded their cars, they headed to a furniture store to buy a bed and kitchen table. It was to be delivered the next day so they spent the night at a hotel on the "Plaza".

The next morning they went grocery shopping and even got paper plates to eat on. Their new furniture was delivered at three and they were very pleased with it. Luckily they had pillows, sheets and blankets from the apartment in Springfield.

In one week Kevin was to report for work so they had time to look around the area and get more acquainted. They bought a few more items for the apartment and Kevin needed a few new clothes for his new job. They found what he needed and he was all set to start work. Terri would not start her new job until fall so she got a part time job as a hostess at lunch time in a really nice restaurant.

She was saving the money she made to buy supplies for her classroom in the fall because Kevin made plenty of money for them to live on and then some. He was designing cell towers for all over the country and really liked what he was doing.

He told Terri that they needed to talk about getting married and she said she wanted to get married in Florida on the beach where they met and Kevin thought that was a fabulous idea.

He wasn't sure what to do about an engagement ring but went to a small jewelry store near where they lived and looked at rings. He decided on one as soon as he saw it and bought it. He called Terri and told her to get dressed up and they were going out to dinner that night to celebrate something big but he wouldn't tell her more than that. She sure was curious but showered and did her hair and chose a cute red dress with black heels and black accessories. She was totally ready when Kevin got home. He told her to give him ten minutes and they would leave for the restaurant. He put on a coat and tie and soon they were headed for the "Plaza" for dinner at a really cool Italian restaurant. He had made a reservation and they had a very cozy table in one of the Italian decorated rooms. He ordered champagne and Terri was surprised after having escargot for an appetizer. Kevin ordered their dinner. Terri kept asking him what was the occasion and he simply told her to be patient and she would find out.

After dinner, he stood up and walked around the table, got down on one knee, professed his love for her and asked her to marry him. She had tears in her eyes and said yes.

She loved the ring and it fit perfectly. Other people in the room started applauding the young couple.

After dinner they went dancing and later went home. Terri was still overwhelmed. Kevin slowly undressed her and laid her on their bed. He slipped off his clothes and they made love two times in the next two hours. Soon they both fell asleep and both dreamed of their happiness.

The next day was Saturday so neither one had to go to work. They slept in and Kevin made a veggie omelet for breakfast. They had a great day together and talked more about a beach wedding.

CHAPTER 46

They had definitely decided on a beach wedding in Destin, Florida and wanted it to be sometime in May. Terri immediately called her parents to tell them and they were all for it.

Then Kevin called his folks and they thought it was a great idea.

Before they knew it, Terri's parents had reserved three condos and a place for the wedding dinner. It was the same restaurant at the country club that Mr. Carter had taken them the week they met.

Terri told Kevin that she wanted Sally and Cat to be in the wedding. Kevin wanted his friend from high school and Jake.

Jake declined due to his financial situation so Kevin decided he wanted his dad to be his best man.

May was approaching fast and the arrangements were being made. Terri found the dress she wanted and sent pictures to her mom. Her mom loved it and told her to buy it. It was a halter dress with a thin lace around her neck and the rest was pretty much free flowing from the waist down.

They had decided that everyone at the wedding should be bare foot except Kevin's grandma and aunt unless they wanted to.

The event was planned for May fifteenth, a Saturday. Everyone was excited about going to Florida for the wedding.

Neither Kevin nor Terri had any problems getting off work for a week. They had decided to fly to Florida and everyone who was coming was also flying. Both Mr. Carter and Mr. Ruble had arranged for large SUV's to rent and Mr. Ruble had rented a convertible for the bride and groom.

Kevin had booked the honeymoon suite for the night of the wedding and two more nights after that.

Soon it was time for all of them to head for their airports. Terri's mom, dad and aunt were all flying together. Kevin's folks, grandma, aunt, Cat and his friend and wife were all flying out of Des Moines. Kevin and Terri left earlier than the rest from Kansas City.

Once they were all there and got their car they headed for the condos. Sally and Roger were on a later flight and Kevin and Terri were going to the airport later to pick them up.

Terri had told Sally to just wear a cute sundress and lots of sunscreen so she wouldn't burn or get too many more freckles.

Terri and the ladies were all at a salon having manicures, pedicures and their hair done. It was a gift from Terri's aunt who thought Terri was like her own child.

Everyone was back at the condos by four and Mr. Carter had a light lunch delivered for everyone.

Then it was time to start getting ready for the wedding. Kevin took a shower, shaved, and styled his hair.

Terri took a quick bath so she wouldn't mess up her hair. She was wearing it down and slightly curled.

Soon it was time and everyone went to the beach. The condo had set up an area for the wedding and it was beautiful. A white rose arrived for Kevin to pin on his white shirt. He was wearing khaki pants, a white shirt and barefoot.

Before Terri's dad walked her to the beach he gave her a beautiful bouquet of white roses and a huge hug and a kiss.

Then they proceeded to the beach.

Kevin was totally overwhelmed when he saw Terri approaching. It was like the first time he saw her and he started to tremble. His dad as best man, noticed and put his hand on Kevin's back and whispered that she was a beautiful bride and told his son how much he loved him and how happy he was to have Terri officially joining the family.

They had a local minister conduct the ceremony and by the time the "I do's" were said almost all were in tears and the sun had started to set. What a beautiful, romantic evening it had been.

Then three large white limos showed up and they all piled in to go to the fancy golf club for dinner.

They had a marvelous dinner, danced some afterwards and then Kevin and Terri left in one of the limos for the hotel.

CHAPTER 47

They had a marvelous wedding night with champagne, chocolate covered strawberries and great sex on a bed of rose petals.

The next day both their families met for breakfast except for Kevin and Terri. They had breakfast from room service.

Kevin's mom and dad dropped the convertible at the hotel for them and briefly had time to hug them and head for the airport to fly home. The Carter's had already left for the airport just in time to catch their flight to St. Louis. The Ruble's plane left an hour later for Des Moines.

Kevin and Terri spent the afternoon on the beach and they even talked about having a family someday. Terri told Kevin that she wanted to wait at least two years so she could have a couple years teaching under her belt and, of course, Kevin agreed with his beloved wife. Terri was now Mrs. Kevin Ruble and she loved it.

They had a great time on their three day honeymoon on the beach but had to catch a flight Tuesday night for Kansas City. Kevin was supposed to work Wednesday but Terri didn't have to go back to the restaurant until Monday.

The two of them had a great summer. They visited his folks and hers each on available weekends.

It was time for school to start and Terri had been going in for teacher's meetings and fixing up her classroom for the first day of school. She decided to let her students sit where they wanted. She knew she could learn their names fast enough without a seating chart.

The students loved that idea and soon all the boys in her room were in love with the teacher and the girls all wanted to hang out with her and be close.

Kevin really got a kick out of all of Terri's stories about her class. Everything was going great for them and exactly as they had planned.

They had their weekends free and did lots of sightseeing in the Kansas City area and enjoyed many of the city's fine restaurants and had gone to a Kansas City Chiefs football game. Their life was perfect for them. They both loved their job and had a really nice income for just starting out.

Soon, Terri was stricken with the flu and did not work for one week. She felt so lousy that she had forgotten to take her birth control pills for four days. She was feeling better and she and Kevin made love that night. It was the weekend so they went out for dinner that night. When they got home, they made love again.

Two months passed and Terri had not had a period. She thought it was due to the flu; when the third month rolled around and no period, she told Kevin. They immediately went to buy a pregnancy test. Low and behold, Terri was definitely pregnant. She made an appointment with her obstetrician that week and the doctor confirmed it and told her that she was probably twelve weeks along.

Kevin and Terri were so excited.

The next morning Kevin suggested they should start looking for a house to buy so they would have room for a family. Terri agreed with his suggestions and they contacted a realtor.

Terri was hoping to make it through the rest of her school year but she knew that it would be close. Her due date was May 25th and this was the same day the last day of school was going to be.

It was a fun spring and their parents were so excited. They visited them often in Kansas City and when Kevin's dad was there, he took him to a house in a small town nearby in Pleasant Hill. His dad thought it would be a good investment and that he should buy it.

Kevin was already approved for the loan so he and Terri bought the house. They closed on it right before Easter and both their parents and Cat came to help them move in.

The two dads went with Kevin to buy blinds for the windows and also split the cost. They took them to the new house and installed them in an hour. The two moms and Terri went looking for baby furniture and came home with a darling bassinet and the rest was to be delivered the next day. The two moms had split the cost so Terri and Kevin weren't out any money except for the house.

Monday morning both sets of parents and Cat headed home. They told their kids how happy they were to become grandparents and Cat told them she would be the best auntie ever.

Terri was getting pretty big with the pregnancy and her students even laughed at her because of her big tummy. They bought a few more things for the house and her. They were all ready for the baby to arrive.

On Monday May 20th Terri was having contractions. Kevin called both parents to tell them and all four parents and Cat were headed for Kansas City early the next day.

Terri called her school and told them what was going on and to get a substitute teacher for the final few days. The school principal was very excited for her.

That night, Terri's water broke at midnight and everyone rushed her to the hospital. They all sat praying and could not wait for the baby to be born.

CHAPTER 48

At ten in the morning on May 22nd, Terri delivered twin boys weighing six and a half pounds each and twenty inches long. It was a huge surprise because they did not know that they were having twins. The boys were identical and they named them Keith and Kurt. The grandparents and Cat were so excited they could not keep from holding the twins and loving on them. Three days later they all took Terri and the twins home. The two grandparents had already gone out and bought another bassinet and a baby bed just like the first one.

The nursery was all set up when the twins arrived and Terri and Kevin were so pleased.

Then next day all went home except for Terri's mom. She stayed to help for a few days. The twins were a handful to manage and it was wonderful that Mrs. Carter stayed on to help. Kevin had to get to work the following Monday and he didn't know how he and Terri would manage without Mrs. Carter.

Kevin's mom came to spend the second week and after that Terri and Kevin were on their own.

They were able to manage pretty well on their own and Kevin was only getting about four hours of sleep a night. He was always up with the boys and let Terri sleep so she could manage on her own during the day.

Cat had graduated high school by then and wanted to come and help with the twins. She wanted to go to college at UMKC. Terri and Kevin relished the idea. So Cat enrolled and got accepted. She would be taking ten hours to start and Terri was going back to teaching the first of November. Cat's schedule worked good with Terri so she and Terri were able to manage at home without extra help.

Kevin was so pleased that Cat had come to live with them and help out. Cat really wanted to major in dance but for now was taking basic classes and an hour of Physical Education. She was happy because she thought Keith and Kurt were the cutest little guys ever.

Thanksgiving arrived and Cat went to Pella to be with her parents. Terri's mom and dad were coming and Terri had bought the turkey and all the trimmings for Thanksgiving dinner. Mrs. Carter got up at five in the morning and put the turkey in to bake. She told Terri to relax and she would take care of the meal. Mr. Carter took turns holding the twins and was having the time of his life.

Christmas came around and all four parents and Cat descended on them. This time Mrs. Ruble cooked and they had prime rib, twice baked potatoes and Mr. Carter made a Caesar salad and Yorkshire pudding. Terri made a wonderful apple cobbler. They all enjoyed the holiday and the twins had so many presents and weren't even old enough to be aware of them.

Cat stayed while all the parents left two days after Christmas. New Year's was quiet and on January first, Terri and Cat took down the Christmas tree while Kevin watched the boys. Kevin and Terri were fantastic parents and both of them gave a great deal of credit to their parents because of how they were raised.

CHAPTER 49

Kevin, Terri, and Cat were all busy with their own schedules and taking turns taking care of the twins. Cat loved living there and being "Auntie Cat". Everything seemed to be working out great.

Terri was back to teaching and she loved her job. She would tell her students stories about the twins every day. The students always inquired as to when the twins would visit their class. So Terri asked Cat to load them in her car and bring them to school. The students were elated and all of them took turns holding them and playing with them. After an hour Terri asked Cat to take the boys home because she had to get back to teaching them some math.

It was a very successful day and when they told Kevin about it that night, he was excited that all went well. He fed the boys their dinner, gave them a bath and put them to bed. Terri fixed dinner and Cat worked on a paper that was due in two days.

The three of them ate dinner together. Cat cleaned up the kitchen and both Kevin and Terri thanked her and told her what a huge help she was being.

Kevin told Cat that she needed to go out socially in the evenings when he and Terri were home. Cat really didn't agree but told him that she would look into it.

Two days later Cat told Kevin she was going with some friends to the student Union to watch "Forrest Gump" in the Union theater. She knew it was one of Kevin's favorite movies and asked him if he would like to join them. Kevin declined because he had more things to do at home with the twins but told her to have a good time.

Cat was surprised but a guy she knew from her English class named Tim asked her to go for a milkshake after the movie. Cat really thought he was cute and accepted the invitation. After that evening they started dating about every weekend. The big surprise was when Cat went to a hair salon and had her hair cut extremely short with lots of fringe bangs and fringe around her face. Tim loved it but when Kevin saw her, he almost fainted. However, he told her that it would grow on him and Terri loved it.

CHAPTER 50

The next surprise in the family was that Terri was pregnant again. Everyone was very excited. The boys were two and here she was expecting a third.

As life went on, a girl was born to Kevin and Terri and they named her Katherine after his grandma and sister, only with a K. They wanted to call her Kathy instead of Cat and the family agreed.

Cat and Tim were graduating soon and were planning a wedding in Pella. Tim was a construction management major and Mr. Ruble offered him a job and Tim was excited to join Cat's family business.

Cat was graduating with a library science degree and the librarian in Pella was retiring so she applied for the job and got it.

They had a wonderful early summer wedding and after a honeymoon cruise they returned to Pella, moved into a two bedroom duplex and started their new careers.

Kevin had been promoted to first vice president in his company and with the money he would be making they decided Terri would teach one more year and then stay home with the kids. They bought a larger home in Pleasant Hill and their life was great.

The Ruble's and the Carter's were headed to Hawaii for a ten day cruise together. Both the Carter's were retired and Mr. Ruble had Tim to run his company and Mrs. Ruble had sold her store for a good price.

Within a year Cat was expecting a child and Tim and her parents could not have been happier.

Kevin, Terri and the three kids were all settled in their new house. Life was good for all.

Printed in the United States
By Bookmasters